NIGHT SEASON

Books by Robert O'Neil Bristow

NIGHT SEASON

TIME FOR GLORY

NIGHT SEASON

Robert O'Neil Bristow

WILLIAM MORROW AND COMPANY

NEW YORK / *1970*

To Cynthia

"O my God, I cry in the daytime, but thou hearest not: and in the night season also I take no rest."

THE BOOK OF COMMON PRAYER

1

The courthouse, of famished yellow stone, too old to be stately anymore, glowed in the dull light of the corner lamps. On the lawn the monument to the confederate dead stood proudly in defeat, casting a weird shadow across the summer grass, resembling more than anything a phallus now. Around the square the business buildings were almost dark inside for the most part, except for a small light to illuminate the interior for a passing policeman. In this South Carolina town of Yorksboro, the hardware store, the cafeteria, the Woolworth's, the J. C. Penney's stood side by side—silent, waiting for tomorrow, the same names on similar courthouse squares in perhaps five hundred Southern towns that were hardly different at all.

Quiet . . . at peace at last. But for a solitary figure making his way unsteadily along the side of the square, down Mount Olive Street. At the corner he paused, weaving slightly, not far from home now. He listened to the small city sleep, a little restlessly perhaps, making strange sounds occasionally, but lulled in slumber.

Toby was pleased. Those many hours before, he had set out to put this rebellious city to bed. And while he walked he told her a story and sang her a lullaby as she grew quiet. He whispered to her then, lovingly, until at three, no, about three-thirty, it was nearly done.

The four-story Palmetto Bank building on the corner was lighted with floodlights but it was dark inside. Every last window was dark. Toby paused at the polished glass doors and looked at himself in the reflection. Touched his dark lips with a finger and smiled foolishly as he gestured his clown-like image to be silent. He pushed his odd little cap toward the middle of his head. The soiled shirt was hanging out of his beltless trousers. He tucked the shirttail in and grinned conspiratorially at himself, weaving again, adjusting his bent gold glasses frames. He spoke softly to the black clown.

"Toby, you want a drink?"

The clown bowed fatuously. "That's kind of you."

He withdrew the pint bottle from his hip pocket, unscrewed the cap, gestured a toast.

"You are a pretty sad mess, Snow. You look like a vagrant."

The face frowned, pained by this, then softened as the neck of the bottle slipped closer to his lips.

It was a quick drink . . . and ghastly. What was it? He could not remember the brand because he had never known for sure. Toby glanced about suspiciously for a police squad car, returning the bottle to his hip pocket. They were the hardest to bed down at night. They only napped occasionally. He could not trust them.

He blew a small kiss to the building and moved along, swaying as though walking the deck of a rolling freighter, down Cashua Street, where the long arms of the streetlights illuminated the entire thing just for him now. In the clothing stores the mannequins stood drowsily, the best-dressed creatures in town. That was really something, wasn't it?

A parade of bubbles traveled along inside the neon tubes of the Piedmont Drug Store sign. The two department stores on Cashua frowned at each other. *I can sell anything you can sell better.*

On the next corner a cab was parked, the motor dead. The driver sat with his head thrown back against the seat. As Toby watched, the driver moved and flung an arm over his eyes. Dreaming, he thought, of a woman in a tight skirt, with a splashy red mouth who spoke to him about love in the back seat. *Sleep now . . .*

He crossed the street, moving south toward the black area. When he reached the theater, he paused before the the huge cardboard faces of two screen lovers whose lips touched in suspended passion. Toby whispered to them, "You can finish it now."

He stood for a moment, his trousers sagging, growing sad, remembering the taste of lips and the smell of perfume and sudden laughter from long ago. Then he walked slowly on with the mood of the lovers following. Death was his silent companion, unobtrusive but ever present.

A block farther south the storefronts were no longer flashy and the window lights cast many deep shadows. Here the pawnshops began, removed from the stores where cherished things were bought new. Here they were sold to a pawnbroker, bitterly or sadly, and sometimes traded for more practical things. Toby had seen fancy guitars traded for revolvers, wedding rings for switchblades.

Across the street the crimson-lettered jewelry store sign offered *Engagement Rings,* a promise of lifetime and love. But below, caged by the glass window, reflecting light a dozen ways, glistened the polished steel-knife blades, promising agony and death.

Next to this was the tired old bookstall where chocolate paint curled to reveal a dead green, which in turn was chipped to reveal a dirty white below, all layers clinging to the rotting wood. Where the proprietor traded one used paperback for two, if there were no pages missing and no lewd drawings scribbled inside the covers.

Now the buildings grew darkly sinister, the shadows looming larger, making huge murky pie slices in the alleys. Toby paused beneath a streetlight and imagined the echo of a lonely clarinet, heard it whirling toward the black sky. The reed was crying softly. All that hot jazz, all those passionate notes were gone. The reed was tired and very sad, now hushed like the moan of a woman growing old in a black satin dress and no man.

And over there behind that dark window, perhaps the tapping of tears falling on bare pillow ticking. Maybe upstairs the bubbling squish of air pushed from a hypodermic syringe. Then the curved spoon, shining gaily over a dancing flame . . . while breakfast cooked.

A rat scampering across the street hesitated to study him for a moment. A large one, gray, intelligent. The rat nodded an abrupt greeting and scurried along, unafraid.

Toby was almost home, moving along slowly under the streetlights that sparkled like distant stars, listening to the clarinet moaning. As he passed the sidewalk mission where the sign promised that *Christ Died For the Ungodly,* he paused to examine the S on the window. It was a good one. He remembered the saying that if a sign painter could make a decent S, he could make a decent living.

Toby admitted modestly that the S was a good one. He had done the sign for two dollars and seventy-five cents, which was not a very good living, but the clergy had asked for an ecclesiastical discount. Later, with that money plus a few cents, Toby had haggled exhaustively until he purchased a fifth of really very bad whiskey, at a sign painter's discount.

He passed the Snug Inn and the adjacent Snug Inn Bar where the girls worked upstairs. Between performances up there, they inhabited the bar, black legs jiggling, thighs winking to attract customers, an arrangement profitable to the management of the bar as well as to the girls. They worked things out down there. *Goodnight, ladies . . .*

He reached at last the business establishment where the glass front was cracked rather badly—so badly a strip of plastic tape ran the entire length of it, holding the two pieces together. Up high on the glass, lettered neatly, was the inscription *Tobias Isaiah Snow Sign Company*, beneath which was printed somewhat steadily, *Signs of Distinction*.

Inside, there were several buckets, a desk, two ladders, and a pot of brushes. In the corner an easel displayed a partly finished canvas, a painting of a black doll with one eye missing, bruised, the hair torn away in places, the clothes ragged and filthy. And the doll was tossed atop a shiny new garbage can. Toby studied it briefly, critically. There were strokes he wanted to make beneath the mouth. He visualized it, considered going inside and doing it, then shrugged and turned away . . . and he wondered why he had gone through four years of college for this—to be a sign painter. But then, he didn't know . . .

Next to the shop was the darkened stairway which he climbed wearily. He stumbled once and felt a splinter gouge his knee. At the top he breathed very heavily, then went along the musty-smelling hallway. *Like a tomb.* At the end of the hall a naked forty-watt bulb glowed, throwing a light that grew quite faint by the time it reached the stairway. The boards beneath his feet creaked with every step, playing a little tune he knew by heart. He listened to it, approving, until he reached his room and went inside, leaving the door open, undressing by a light from the alley that illuminated the rear door of the used clothing store, an angry 250-watt thing. He frowned at it, tossing his shirt and slacks toward, but not quite reaching, a chair. He heard the bottle thud on the floor and winced.

"I have," he said, weaving, "killed my friend."

In the near darkness he felt around the floor for the trousers, found the bulge in the pocket, and withdrew the bottle. It was not broken or cracked. It did not even leak. He carried it to his shelf of valuables—an open-faced fruit box nailed to the wall—and deposited it there. Sighing deeply, he snapped the elastic of his shorts and removed the bridge from his mouth, placing the two front teeth on the table beneath the box. Then he got into bed and wondered if it was worth the effort to untie his shoes. Somehow the thought got lost and he had a vague feeling that he had forgotten something important.

The light from the alley was in his eyes. He closed them and tried to fall asleep without thinking . . . thinking . . . about the light out there in the alley shining viciously in his eyes. *Won't he ever understand?* It was hopeless. He tried covering his eyes with the pillow, but it occurred to him that he might smother. He groaned aloud.

"It must be done," he said to himself, "over and over until he understands."

He rolled out of the bed and felt uncertainly about the corner of the room, finding the baseball bat, searching on until he located the BB gun. Squatting on the floor under the window, bracing the barrel on the sill, he cocked the gun, rolling the BB's around inside. He smiled sleepily.

It was very quiet now. A gentle breeze moved through the window. He saw two barrels and two lights and could not decide which light to aim at. His head bobbed and he shook himself awake, aiming the rifle at what seemed to be the real bulb, and squeezed, ever so gently . . . and bang!

He had missed it. There was a pinging sound when the BB hit the metal *Used Clothing Store* sign directly behind the light. *That was all right. Yes, sir. That was close for the first shot.*

As he rolled the pellets around inside the barrel and cocked again, he heard the sounds along the alley. From an open window a man's voice groaned and cursed softly. From behind him he heard Roxanne begin to stir. He fired again. *Bang* . . . then, *ping.*

He blinked sleepily. It would be good if it did not take too long. He was falling asleep at the window with the damned light burning right in his face. He couldn't do that. He heard the door down the hall swing open and the bare feet on the floor.

"What you doin'?" Her voice was almost unintelligible with sleep. And he heard Roxanne answering herself, "He's got that goddam kid gun again." Her feet shuffled into the room behind him. "Toby . . . hell, it's four o'clock!"

He nodded, not looking back, and cocked the air rifle a third time.

"You won't quit," she said.

". . . of a bitch," came a voice from another room.

"Toby . . ."

He squeezed the shot and missed again. Roxanne moaned. He smelled her when she came near, a gardenia odor, but there was that other smell of douche . . . the antiseptic cleanliness one associates with clean whores when the day's work is done. She knelt beside him and he pointed the gun again, feeling her hair on his arm. She was looking down the barrel with him. He missed again.

"Want to try?" he asked generously.

"Couldn't you put a shade on the window?" she asked.

"Too hot." The exhaustion was coming to his arms and his eyes were burning, very dry from aiming at the light.

"Then aim careful," she encouraged, accepting the necessity of the war but longing for an early victory.

"Sometimes I feel like I'll hit it and I do."

"Feel that way then."

He smiled tolerantly. She did not understand either. Toby summoned courage. He called upon some inner strength and eyed down the barrel, blinking rapidly, and carefully began to pull the trigger. *You can't jerk it . . . you can't rush it or you tighten and miss badly. You must squeeze slowly . . .* and saw in the blinding light the bodies of men rotting in the jungles. Saw the villages burned and gutted. Smelled the odor of decay of once-living beings who laughed and who wept and who wanted desperately to live, to trace the face of a woman with fingertips and fill glasses with whiskey and shout joyously, *I live! I live!* Fallen in hand-to-hand combat. Enemies lying immobile, embracing each other. Peace at last.

You must squeeze slowly . . . think something else. Anything else. Count . . . recite something foolish . . . Greater love hath no man than this . . . that a man lay down his life . . .

The rifle fired and in the next instant the bulb shattered, appearing to grow extremely bright at first before it sizzled, yielding to the great darkness and defeat, as the glass tinkled like an expensive little bell, falling to the bottom of the pole, clinking musically as it came to rest on last night's glass . . .

He lowered his head against the gunstock and blinked, his eyes burning. Roxanne touched his chest.

"Now go to bed, Toby . . . for God's sake." She stood. "Get up. I'll help you," she said. She took his arm and hugged it against her and he felt the curve of her breast.

He let her put him to bed but he still did not remove his shoes. "Goodnight, Toby," she said and went down the hall.

He heard the floor creak and closed his eyes. The world began to rotate and with great effort he turned over on his stomach. Toby listened. He heard the distant note of the clarinet drop low, hushed, vibrating like the idling engine of an interstate truck as the driver paused to wipe his eyes.

His jaw muscles relaxed and his lips parted slightly. As his mind cleared somewhat, he heard the doctor's voice again, like the voice of a police officer, a tone that sounded like an ultimatum—which it was, he supposed. He was lying on the white table and he felt the white hand probing along his black belly. The doctor turned away and told Toby to get dressed. When he was finished, the doctor sat on a stool and motioned him to a chair beside a table cluttered with bottles and instruments.

"You've had a heart attack. When was it?" he asked, running the strip of long, narrow paper through his hands slowly, frowning, making his lips tighten into a neat little line which the white moustache paralleled. Toby did not answer. He didn't really know. The doctor still studied the electrocardiogram. "Who treated you?"

"Nobody. I didn't know."

The doctor clipped the paper to his folder and looked up slowly, curiously. "You'd have to know," he said.

Toby moistened his lips. Was he supposed to argue with the man? "I hurt sometimes," he said. "Never bad."

"How much do you drink a day?"

Toby reached for a cigarette.

"I'd rather you didn't do that," the doctor said. "It isn't good for you."

Toby frowned. He was not very steady and he could have used a cigarette, but he let his hand drop to the table. He

let out a long sigh that was something of a shudder. "A fifth
. . . maybe a quart some days."

The doctor blinked but he did not show a judgment in his
face. "How long have you been doing this?"

"It wasn't always that much . . . the last few years . . .
but not every day, not always."

"What do you drink?"

"This and that . . ."

"Cheap liquor?"

"Well"—he smiled and automatically reached for the cigarette again before he remembered—"I don't drink Jack
Daniels."

The doctor found no humor to that.

"Vodka . . . a lot of that."

The doctor nodded and lighted a cigarette himself, though
his manner indicated that it would not be acceptable for
Toby to join him. "All right, Mr. Snow . . ."

Toby smiled. They didn't used to say that down here.
Maybe they called them by the first name or sometimes
even "boy," but things had changed.

". . . here's the way it is. I'm going to give you two prescriptions. The first one will be a sedative. That's to relax you
so that you can get over this liquor binge. Don't drink when
you take these or you may never wake up." He began to
write as he spoke, quite businesslike now. "The other prescription is for pain in the chest. If you feel any pain at all,
slip one of these under your tongue and sit down. In the
street, if you have to, but stop. You're not in good shape, Mr.
Snow. You ought to go home and get in bed for at least a
week. Can you do that?"

Toby nodded.

The doctor ripped the pages from the prescription pad.
"Then . . . there is the liver. Two-thirds of your liver is
gone. If you stop drinking entirely and stop smoking and

get plenty of rest, avoid strain . . . you have some time. If you don't, it's a question of whether your heart gets you first or your liver. Either way . . ." He handed Toby the slips of paper. "That's all I can do," he said.

Toby nodded again and came to his feet. His legs were not very steady. He went to the door and when he turned the doctor was looking at him, exhaling slowly.

Outside, Levi was waiting in the cab, chewing Dentyne vigorously, his big belly hanging over his belt. Toby got into the cab. "What did he say?" Levi asked. The moon face was glistening with sweat and Toby watched the jaws work fiercely with the gum.

Toby shrugged. "He gave me some medicine. I've got to stop by the drugstore on the way back."

"Yeah."

Levi took him to the Fidelity Drug Store and the pharmacist glanced at him, looked at the prescriptions, and began to jerk bottles from the shelf.

"What's in the pills?" Toby asked.

The pharmacist did not look up. Toby could hear the pills rattling as he poured them onto his work counter. "One to relax you. The other to stop chest pain. You've got a heart condition?"

"That's what he said."

"Then you have. Keep this bottle in your pocket all the time. If you forget them, go back after them. You don't know when you'll need one."

Goddammit, hand me a shovel and I'll start digging to save time.

He paid for the drugs and Levi took him home. When he climbed the stairway he could feel the breathlessness and the pounding but that was the way it always was the next morning. When he got his breath, he was all right. He put the pills in the fruit box and stretched out on the bed. In a little while he was breathing all right.

So a man had to think about it a little bit. He reached under his pillow and withdrew the bottle, lifting his head to avoid spilling it, and swallowed twice. He screwed the cap back on the bottle and placed it carefully beside the bed. Yes, a man had to think about that pretty good. He couldn't just jump up from the white table and slap twenty greens into the doctor's hand and run out and not take another one again . . . because at forty-three there wasn't as much to the women anymore, especially when he was drunk, and Roxanne always wanted to be good to him like that, but he didn't want to pay her like the others did because it wasn't any good that way, and he felt he ought not to use her if he didn't pay, though she never said anything about it. And long ago he knew that there would be nothing for him but painting signs, that the other thing, that dream before his hands began to shake so much in the morning, that idea that he could put something down that people would look at and maybe feel something . . . that soul thing. Well, it hadn't happened, at least not very often, when somebody took the hard cash and went away with a painting. All those art contests, when he took his entry and hoped and was always disappointed when the judges gave the prizes to the colorful blobs and geometric designs, failing to understand that he was trying to show them something real, like it really was. So he didn't enter them anymore and—except for Roxanne who praised his work so that it spoiled it; she put on too much—nobody really noticed.

A man had to think about that decision hard because what was left after forty . . . He breathed deeply and was almost pleased with the idea that drifted through his mind and knew it could not be original, knew that some black preacher had probably said it years ago . . . that the road got narrower every day until there was hardly room to walk, and all around, on either side, there was nothing but darkness and someday the darkness came up in front of you and you just stopped and stood waiting, knowing that the next step would take you there and that was all.

He was afraid of it. There was that thing inside that maybe God put there, that a man doesn't rush it, that he walks that narrowing road slower so it takes more time to get to the narrow part. A liver. Maybe two-thirds gone. If God had known man was about to invent liquor he should have given him two livers. He knew he had to pee, so he gave him two kidneys. Why didn't he know a man had to drink? The whole thing didn't make sense.

Now his shoes were hurting his feet. He wished he had asked Roxanne to take them off. The feet would be swollen tomorrow.

Okay, then. What had his son looked like inside that box when they brought him back? What was under that flag?

No. Not now, baby.

Toby could feel the sleep coming. It would come suddenly and then it would be tomorrow. He had put the little city to bed. And the policeman hadn't taken him in. What more could a man ask? And that other thing, he could think about that later. It had taken twenty years. There ought to be no big hurry now. He surrendered to the night.

2

The heat came with the morning, bearing the aroma of the alley, a damp, heavy odor of the sewer, the decay of garbage. There came pain also. The ache seemed everywhere at once but especially favored his feet. Raising them to eye level, he saw the toes of his shoes and remembered vaguely that before he slept he had intended to remove them but the effort had been too great.

His legs were like wooden stumps. He began to move his toes inside the shoes to stimulate the circulation. This brought a new and different pain, a prickly sensation. He heard a radio playing down the hall and moved his toes in an agony of rhythm. Soon this difficulty passed and he was able to concentrate on the pain in his head, which throbbed severely. A part of his tongue had stuck to the roof of his mouth because he had slept with his mouth open. He rattled the tongue about his mouth, seeking moisture in some secluded crevice, describing the peaks of molar mountains whose valleys suffered drought.

A tall pitcher of ice water. He visualized it, imagined

pouring some into a glass, and even heard the slivers of ice sliding over the lip, splashing into the pool.

Then he heard her voice from across the hall. "I tore my goddam hose. How'd I tear it? How do I always manage to tear hose?"

Why does a black whore worry about hose? He fell asleep briefly—not a real sleep but a dull semiconsciousness interrupted by the cursing in the alley. So thorough and bitter it was, Toby turned his head and looked down where Woodrow Prince paced back and forth kicking the pieces of broken glass.

"Ninety-eight goddam cents," pounding a round fist against his heart, "ninety-eight cents it costs me to put in the light so the thieves won't carry the store away. And this idiot . . . this drunken bastard . . ." At which time he turned abruptly, his fat short body swaying, and pointed an accusing finger up . . . up to the window where Toby watched. "You got no respect for the law, Toby Snow. Twenty-five . . . goddammit, twenty-five *hundred* times I put in this light and you shoot it out. Only *this* time I got enough. This time the law is going to hear and I hope they put your worthless ass in jail for ten lousy years. Do you hear me, Snow?"

Words of reply came to Toby's mind and to his mouth but the words did not form because he was out of spit and his tongue would not move properly. *I hear you and the people down the block hear you. I think even God hears you.* He was sorry he was not able to say it because he liked it very much.

"You think . . ." Woodrow came closer under the window, shaking his fist angrily. "You think you can do this forever and I won't call the cops. You been takin' advantage of my good nature too long. Right now I'm gonna call the cops and I hope they put your worthless ass in jail for ten lousy years." The fat figure waddled out of the alley into the rear door of the used clothing store.

As Toby turned away, Roxanne moved in the doorway, leaning against it. She wore a pair of slacks and a brassiere and looked like a light chocolate Playboy bunny. The brassiere was terrific, the cleavage making a creamy bulging crevice. "You took terrible," she said, surveying the disaster.

His tongue would not loosen for her either. He slid his feet carefully off the bed and got up in measured stages, slowly, and shuffled stiffly toward the sink. He drew his trousers from the floor and, leaning against the wall, stepped into them. Bending over the sink, he turned on the tap and sloshed water in his face, cupping his hands and drinking from them. But it was not cool and sweet as he had imagined. It tasted like rusting pipes and it was yellow and it did not make him feel very much better.

"He'll really call the cops," Roxanne said. She drew a filter cigarette to her lips, holding it between long exquisite fingers.

Toby nodded, carefully moving past her to the orange crate where he located the bottle. There was one *very* good drink or two *fairly* good drinks in the pint. He opened it, squeezed his eyes tight, and took one very good drink. Then holding the empty, blinking rapidly, swallowing hurriedly, he kept it down. He tossed the empty into the trash area, a corner near the door, and began to search for his teeth. Turning his back on Roxanne, hunching his shoulders secretively, he slipped the bridge into place.

"I figured out some strokes," he said, "around the mouth and eyes of the doll. That's where it was wrong."

"What the hell are you talking about?"

"They need to be sad," he said to himself. He bent over, took his shirt out of the trash pile, and slipped it on. A package of crushed cigarettes peeped from the pocket. He took one, put it in his mouth, and forgot about it.

"He's calling the cops," Roxanne said.

"Okay." The cigarette bobbed. Toby sat wearily on the bed. "The city was nice. It was very quiet," he said.

"It wasn't so quiet once you started with that kid gun, I'll tell you that."

He got up and returned to the sink to drink again. The water had improved. He began to search for a match. "Nobody knows a city unless he walks it at night. That's right, Roxie. *Nobody* does."

She considered this briefly. He smiled because Roxie would not bother to walk the streets of heaven on a nice day.

There were sluggish footsteps in the hall. Levi pushed his face into the doorway. Levi had not shaved. He wore his pajamas and his hat. Levi Duvall had seldom been seen on his feet without the hat he wore while driving his cab.

"Toby, I think that old fart called the cops. He's mad as hell about them lights out there. You better beat it for an hour or something."

Toby sat back on the bed and looked at them thoughtfully, his head splitting, a tightness in his chest, and trembling all over.

"Come on down to the joint and I'll buy us a beer until Woodrow cools off," Levi offered. "I swear he's called the cops."

The cigarette shook as though he were holding an excited worm. Levi struck a match for him and hunted down the tip of the cigarette. It tasted very bad. When Toby did not reply to warnings about the police, they discussed him objectively in the doorway.

"Was he pretty drunk?" Levi asked.

"Well . . . he wasn't in no shape to walk a tightrope, but I've seen him worse."

"What was he drinking?"

"That rotgut he buys. That stuff is terrible."

He heard the sound of voices from the stairway growing louder as they approached. Levi came across the room and took Toby's arm, but Toby resisted.

"That's Woodrow . . . he's got a cop," Levi warned.

"All right."

"All right, my ass. You want to go to jail?"

Toby shrugged.

"Get down to my room before . . ."

"No."

From the hallway, in agitation, "Week after week he does it. He takes a gun, a *firearm*, Officer, and he actually shoots it out. You seen the glass . . . a dollar every time he gets drunk. One dollar. How long I got to put up with that?" Anger had inflated the price of the bulb two cents.

"We'll talk to him. You didn't *see* him do this?"

"No . . . my God, it's three, four o'clock in the fucking morning. You think I can sit out there all night to watch over a goddam light globe?"

They appeared in the doorway. Woodrow was breathing heavily, his face flushed. The officer was Charles Holstead who had done a very good job on the beat by trying to understand that these creatures were people and not wild animals. Few envied Charles Holstead's job. For a Southern cop, Holstead was a saint.

Roxie became sullen, the customary attitude for a prostitute to take in the presence of the law. Levi frowned, unpleasant now, since his own scheme might have prevented the encounter entirely.

"Toby . . ." Officer Holstead began amicably, "Woodrow here says you shot out his light bulb. Is that so?" The officer shifted his weight self-consciously.

It was an incredible accusation. It was actually embarrassing. A grown man accusing another of shooting out a light bulb.

"Well . . ."

Roxie swelled her breasts offensively, which was a disconcerting thing to do. Holstead averted his eyes but not immediately. "Look," she said, "it so happens this fat little bastard has it in for Toby. As a matter of fact," she was pointing a sharp finger at Woodrow Prince, "*I* was with Toby last night. All night long, see, and he did a lot of things but one of them wasn't shooting out no streetlights. That much I can tell you for a *fact*."

Officer Holstead was impressed, Toby thought. Anyway *he* was. Holstead turned toward him for verification of this vital testimony just as Levi began to volunteer his own version.

"They was in my cab. First we had a few beers. When it got late, we drove around for a fare or two and then I brung 'em home. Right here." Levi pointed with his hand to the very spot. Holstead was studying the pajamas and the hat cocked belligerently now atop the thinning hair. Once again he turned to Toby for verification. But before Toby could speak, Woodrow took the floor for the prosecution.

"You think maybe them bulbs come with a explosive made inside? Like every time they get turned on, they blow out and the glass falls in the goddam alley?"

Toby wondered what Westinghouse would say to such an idea.

"I'll tell you, this is a bunch of lies," Woodrow continued. "He shot out them lights and he done it with that gun right over there in the corner."

Toby followed Officer Holstead's eyes to the gun. It looked terribly menacing for a BB gun. It looked like a very guilty gun.

"Toby, what *do* you do with that gun?" Holstead asked.

"He shoots rats," Roxanne said. "There's rats as big as a douche bag loose in this place."

"That's right," Levi agreed.

"It's a lie. He never shot a rat in his life. He *likes* rats."

Toby moistened his lips. "I like rats," he said agreeably. Each appeared to consider this significant.

"One question. That's all. And everybody let Toby answer it," Holstead said officially. "Okay?"

Toby nodded.

"Nobody has ever seen you shoot out those bulbs. You apparently were with *them* last night." He gestured with his thumb to Roxie and Levi. "So I'm asking you, did you or did you not shoot out the bulb?"

Their faces were intent upon him. It was incredible. *Who killed Cock Robin?* He grinned crookedly. "I killed Cock Robin," he said, sharing his wit.

"For Christ's sweet . . ."

"I told you he was with me all night."

"He's lying. He didn't kill nobody. He shot out my *bulb*."

"Okay! Now shut up, everybody. I'll ask you one more time. Did you shoot out that light?"

Toby sighed. "Yes."

The faces drooped. All of them except Woodrow's face. "Are you sure?" Holstead asked, unwilling to accept a confession.

Toby considered that briefly. "Yes," he said.

Holstead turned to Woodrow almost angrily. "You want to file charges? That's what you really want?"

Woodrow seemed unable to collect himself. Apparently he had not for a moment considered that Toby would admit to the charge. "What I want is for him to pay me," he said finally. "I don't want no trouble. I like him, but he's cost me a dollar every time he shoots . . . he ought to pay for the bulbs and never shoot no more."

"Okay, Toby? You'll pay for the bulbs?"

Toby got up and went to the table and got a fresh package of cigarettes and searched around in the orange crate until he located the pills. "No . . ."

Holstead turned to Woodrow and flipped his hand over. "He won't pay. You want to file charges?"

"Well . . . he could pay a little. I mean, for God's sake, this is destruction of private property and firing a dangerous weapon inside the city limits. He could get a year maybe for something serious like that, so if he pays for that *one* light and never shoots no more, then . . ."

"No," Toby said.

Levi stepped forward, jerked a roll of bills from his pocket, tore one off, wadded it up, and threw it on the floor. "There's your lousy buck."

"And he won't shoot no more?" Woodrow asked, sensing victory.

Toby straightened his shoulders. "I'll shoot out every light that gets screwed into that thing as long as it shines in my eyes when I try to sleep."

And this was too much. "You sorry . . . You no-good, worthless . . . Yeah, you take him down to the station and I'll press charges and I hope they lock his worthless ass in jail for ten lousy years."

Toby winced. He had been afraid Woodrow would say it that way again. Roxanne shook her head. "He's nuts. He's hung over and sick and he don't know what he's saying."

"Let's go, Toby," Holstead said softly.

"Okay."

"You'll be sorry for this," Roxie shouted, inches from Woodrow's nose.

Toby walked along the hallway, descending the stairs carefully on very rubbery legs. At the bottom of the stairs he turned to Holstead. "Let me see if the door to the shop is locked." He shuffled to the door, tried it, and stood briefly studying the face of the ragged doll, agreeing that he needed to make some strokes about the mouth.

Holstead waited until he was finished. Then he led him to the patrol car. The people on the street, as though drawn magnetically, seemed to close in. Toby heard voices. "What's Toby done?" And "Hey, Toby, what's happened?" He got into the squad car in order to sit down. His hands were shaking terribly. It was going to be an awful day.

And the old black woman who worked in the cafe came over, wiping her brow with an apron, and peered myopically into the car. Her voice was intimately low. "Toby . . . it ain't bad, is it?"

He placed his hand on hers, stroking the wrinkled flesh gently. "It's nothing," he said.

Roxanne and Levi and Woodrow now appeared at the foot of the stairs as Officer Holstead hesitated. They were arguing vigorously. Holstead rubbed his clean-shaven jaw. Roxanne shook a menacing fist in Woodrow's face. She still wore only her brassiere above the waist and, standing as she did on the bottom step, was in full view of passing traffic. Holstead spoke to her, waving indignantly at the street. She was a safety hazard. Toby read her lips, an obscene reference to the people and to the traffic. Holstead removed his cap and worked intently at wiping nonexistent sweat from the band. A fiasco. A nigger street rumble with the citizenry very much involved. *Your trouble is my trouble, brother.*

"A heap of goddam ashes . . ." Roxanne was saying to Woodrow.

"No . . . no . . ." Holstead was saying.

Woodrow was swallowing hard, his expression one of internal turmoil. Toby blinked in the bright sunlight and rubbed his eyes, a feeble attempt to soothe the pain originating behind them. The crowd converged on Woodrow, who could only retreat back up the stairs. But he stood his ground, arguing fiercely, ". . . every time, a dollar . . ." His face was puffy now and the eyes had taken on an expression of hopelessness.

Levi began to jab his finger into the fat man's chest as he raised his voice. The mangy crowd lobbied in behalf of one of its own. The matter was negotiated.

"Not ever shoot the gun . . ."

"Cover the light . . . fix it so's . . ."

"No more bulbs shot out in . . ."

". . . out of his eyes, for Christ's sake . . ."

"Okay, leave me the hell alone."

"You are not pressing charges?" At last, the official clarification.

"That's right."

At which point the fat body was allowed to escape the thrusting fingers and angry faces and jutting brassiere which had righteously conducted the trial. Toby watched Woodrow pass angrily toward the doorway of the used clothing store, muttering oaths, trembling, breathing hard. And he saw the faces turn toward the squad car where he still sat. Officer Holstead appeared at the door and opened it, not saying a word, weary now of the whole thing.

Toby climbed out and silently offered thanks to his benefactors for this display of unity. They had kept him from the damp, cool walls of the city jail. He followed Roxie's bare shoulders as she mounted the stairs before him and he received Levi's congratulations for, as far as he was responsible, absolutely nothing. He returned to his room, hearing the sounds of rejoicing from the committee for the defense ringing out along the hallway. Until, in a few minutes, peace returned.

He made his way to the bed where he sat down and wished that, after all, he had decided to have two fairly good drinks from the bottle instead of the one good one. He had the splendid idea, now that it was all over, to remove his shoes. He slipped the toe of one shoe against the heel of the other and pushed mightily until the one slipped free and slid across the wooden floor noisily. The second shoe he pulled to his knee and shoved with the heel of his hand. It came free and he let it drop.

Toby stretched his body the length of the bed. As a dullness gathered about his brain, he thought he ought to have a drink of water but declined because the drink that soothed his burned throat activated his resting kidneys. Thus, he sacrificed, closed his eyes, and breathed deeply and unevenly.

The angry brassiere sped across his eyelids and the stubby finger of the cabdriver kept a rhythmic beat, directing a chorus of angry voices. It had been exhausting. In a few minutes Roxanne came in. She stood over him, glowering victoriously. "Baby?" he said softly.

"Yes."

"Come hold me."

"You mean you want it?"

"No, baby. Just lie with me."

She was a pro . . . she knew nothing else. She slipped the brassiere off and the breasts tumbled forward and the nipples, those large round things, not the little tips, lunged forward, free of the restraint. Toby smiled and she came to him.

"You want me to take it all off?"

"No, baby . . . just be close to me for a while."

"Because of the jail?"

"No, because I need you now. Just now."

And so she crept to the bed with her slacks on and no brassiere and pushed her body against him until he felt the warmth and felt comforted against that narrowing road. And there was nothing else. Soon he slept.

3

He sat at the easel in the sign shop, his hands steady now, lettering the sale signs for Wannamaker's Department Store. The pint bottle was on the floor beside his stool and he was working automatically ... LADIES' DRESSES—ONE-HALF PRICE ... the paint sliding, appearing from the brush to the cardboard smoothly as he turned the brush in his fingers before dipping into the paint again. He was dull but his nerves were all right now, even though the pint was low and he'd have to get another one to see him through the day. Because his pants were tight, he had put the bottle of pills on the table beside the paint, a thing Roxanne noticed when she came down.

"I got an allergy," he said. She stroked his neck while he worked until he told her that he couldn't paint signs with a woman rubbing his neck and sending sensations down to his loins, a remark she seemed to appreciate.

In a few minutes she left and he reached for the bottle and took a sip, not a big drink now, just enough to keep his hands loose. He was putting a finished sign aside to dry on the table when Curtis Sadler, the kid, came in, wiping his thin face with a handkerchief. Toby turned to observe Curtis. It never ceased to confuse him, the way Curtis lived up there in that oven above the bar and the poolroom and the grocery store, right in the middle of the black section off New Hope Street, a white boy like that, out of college and able to get a good job, maybe in sociology, which he taught out at the black junior college. The odd thing was he wasn't a Northern boy either, like those kids who came down with the VISTA units to save the black man from God knows what they had in their minds before they arrived. No, Curtis was a Southern boy, from South Carolina, with a Master's in sociology, and he was taking a miserable salary to go down there and teach, which was queer enough, but that still didn't give him any reason to live upstairs with them, with the noise of the bar going on down below and Roxie hauling johns up the stairs at all hours, and bearing the heat, though he did have a small electric fan. Toby studied the unruly blond hair combed down over his forehead in the current style, the long, narrow face accented with pale blue eyes. Curtis didn't look twenty-five, but maybe when a man reached forty-three he didn't have the ability to tell anymore, because twenty-five is a long way to forty-three, or so it seemed. The kid wore slacks with an elastic band and a short-sleeved turtleneck shirt from which hung skinny arms.

"Morning, Toby," he said.

Toby nodded and placed a clean sheet of cardboard on the easel. "Big Curtis, the wonder kid," he said but not unkindly.

Curtis came on in and pulled up a chair. "I don't want to bother you," he said.

"Just don't stroke my neck," Toby said.

"What?"

"Nothing. How's school?"

There was such a long pause that Toby hesitated in his lettering to glance to his left into the kid's face. Curtis had turned the chair around to lean his hands on the back with his chin on his hands. He looked troubled; the brows drew down and the pale blueness beneath clouded. "Sometimes I feel . . ."

Toby turned back to his work. It would come now, like it always did, like it did with all of them.

". . . like it's hopeless."

Toby lettered carefully, dipping for more paint. "Yeah," he said, knowing that was all that was required.

"Toby . . . the only way, the *only* way we can make it is together. I know there can't be two systems. Even if a lot of people got killed, the system isn't going to change that much. They've got to understand that integration is the only answer and that the only way to make it is to learn, to be able to go out and do a job. You know?"

Toby agreed without pausing. It was getting hot as God knew what on the street and the heat was drifting from the asphalt to Curtis's back and, thin as he was, sweat was moistening his shirt.

"But something is happening. I go into class and the students aren't listening. Two years ago maybe they were listening. I don't know. Listen, Toby . . . industry is crying for good talented black people. I made a survey and I've read all about the willingness for industry to hire black executives or good black stenographers or good black plumbers . . . the opportunity is there now."

"That's good," Toby said. "That's a good sign."

He decided he wanted another small drink. He offered the bottle to Curtis, but a pained expression came over the kid's face. "It's not even noon yet," he said.

Toby unscrewed the cap and tasted the liquor briefly, replacing it carefully on the floor, noting that only a third remained. He grew suspicious of himself and turned to examine the last sign he had finished. It was all right. He was pacing himself well.

"Maybe they resent my being white. I don't know why they would. Why, I could be making . . ."

Toby did not turn. He waited for that little note, like a musical sound, that meant self-pity, but it did not follow.

"Some of them have been reading that militant literature. I don't know who's distributing it, but all that about the churches paying a lot of money for reparations and taking over Mississippi and Alabama and Georgia and . . . it's crazy."

Toby stroked with the brush efficiently. "Yes," he agreed, "it is. Mississippi they might get a deal on. But Georgia and Alabama and South Carolina . . . I just don't rightly believe they'll ever be able to swing that."

"I'm serious, Toby."

The tone indicated that Toby had ridiculed him in some way. Toby patiently put down the brush and turned on the stool. He lighted a cigarette with steady hands as the sounds from the street crept into the small shop, the raucous laughter from some black woman who had thrown her head back at the sky and sprung her jaws wide, the sound of the little scratch-off when the black man working at the mill on the next shift (getting a beer or two in preparation) slapped the accelerator and made the tires spin on that new Camero. He could almost hear, or imagined he could, the overhead fans whirling at the pool hall and the click, click of the balls up and down the tables and the whispering hiss as a can of beer was opened . . . the sound of white dice in black hands in the back room behind the pool hall . . . the distant ring of the cash register in the little grocery . . .

He spoke slowly. "You made one mistake, Curtis. What you've done is refer to *all* those students. You put them in one big heap, you see. And that's as bad as the white man used to do in this country down here. He used to say niggers

. . . they all no-good, lazy, no-count. But a man can't do that. No more than we have a right to look at the white man and say that's the man . . . you see, *the man* . . . because there are the rednecks and the honkeys and . . . it just doesn't fit everybody. What you've got to do, Curtis boy, is go back to that class and look into the faces of those kids and you'll see that they aren't *all* asleep. You can't lift *all* our people. You can inspire some of them. I learned that in college too, a philosophy class. Teacher was a big fat nigger with a thick moustache because he was ashamed of his lip, but he taught some pretty good logic and he said the fallacy was that you can't go from *some* to *all* without stumbling."

"Yes . . . I know. I don't suppose I meant it that way really."

"Of course not," Toby said. "Now this business of being white. That's something you can't help. And there are kids in there who never had a white teacher before. They can't look a white man in the eye. Then . . ." He extended his hand, feeling better after that last sip. "You've got, like you said, the kids who think they have to have a black nation, that there ain't no way to make it with the white man, which is sweet dream stuff to some of them. What you've got with them is a need to be somebody. If a man says something really crazy, there is always somebody as crazy as he is who goes along. Curtis," he said expansively, "what you got to do is cool down and do your thing . . ."

"Are you an Uncle Tom?"

Toby laughed. "That's part of the trouble, Curtis. You see, you got to either be an Uncle Tom or you got to be willing to burn down the town. Those folks making all the noise, those people wanting guns . . . you don't seem to hear the people who just go on about their business and do what they have to do, what they can do, and maybe suffer some and maybe not . . . and drink a little whiskey on Saturday night and, hell, get out and cut a strange piece, and Monday go back to work . . . I'm not an Uncle Tom but I'm not going to burn down the town either. I'm Toby. Everybody knows Toby. Toby paints signs. He makes a living. He's got a disability check from the government from World War Two. He drinks a little whiskey and he gets along. See, Curtis, I'm just trying to live." Out of the corner of his eye he saw the bottle of pills and he had a momentary bad feeling. "Toby's not uptight. If you want to go down to teach those kids at the college and some white man calls you a nigger-lover, it's the same thing. He's trying to push you into a corner because labels are always easier to deal with than the facts." He put out his cigarette against the easel and turned slowly back to his sign, dipping the brush into the paint and twisting it smoothly in his fingers.

"I get discouraged," Curtis said.

"Yeah . . . everybody does. The trouble with the world today is something I read the other night when I couldn't sleep. Instant gratification. Everybody wants it *now*. It's all too fast, this world. Man don't take it easy. He don't know patience from shit." He began to paint the letters again, adjusting himself on the stool for more comfort. "A kid today comes out and wants to grab the world by the ass and run off with it. He thinks he's gonna tear it up. Gonna make some kind of world's record. But he don't. And when he's thirty, he looks around and figures out he ain't got it yet. He's got something, but he hasn't set the record . . . so he hustles his ass off and when he's forty, he looks around again and about that time he starts to settle for what he did get . . . But when he's twenty, he wants it all now. He gets out of college and he wants an executive office with the president of the company soliciting his advice on every move. It doesn't occur to him he just might have to work his ass off to prove he's got what it takes. See this sign?" He did not wait for a reply. He was going so good he just rode right on by. "That man called me up and asked me to paint these signs for his sale because he knows I can do the job. But he had to find that out, and that took a little time. Doctor comes to town, hell, he sits there on his hands for a while before he gets somebody cured, and then little by little it starts to happen . . . and in five years you got to call two days ahead to get an appointment. The only instant gratification I know of is masturbation." He leaned suddenly, almost losing his balance, and snapped the bottle by the neck and took a quick drink.

"You're right, you know," Curtis said.

"You know what you need?" Toby asked.

"What?"

"You need to finish those classes on Friday and get all dressed up and go to Charlotte and have a few drinks and find you some gal and cut her. Get a hotel room and keep a bottle up there and just cut her good until you ain't got nothing left."

"I don't know any girls. I don't even know any girls here in Yorksboro."

"That's from spending all your time down here with niggers."

"I don't use that word."

"Words don't hurt people. Then go to Roxie."

"I couldn't pay for it if I did."

"Well, Roxie ain't likely to get cut by hardly anybody unless he's got the money, so you got a problem there." Then he thought, if *he* had paid her, if he had asked her up there and actually paid her what she charged them, how much it would have cost him over the past couple of years, and he had to smile, but then that was something else that Curtis wouldn't understand.

"I don't think that's the answer," Curtis said.

"Maybe not." He finished the sign and put it on top of the last one, now dry.

"I just have to try harder. I have to reach them."

"All right."

"I hate to go upstairs. It's very hot."

"Go in the bar. It's air-conditioned."

"I can't drink. I never could."

"Have a soda pop."

"They give me funny looks when I do that. They make it off beer."

"Then buy a beer and sit there and watch it get warm." Toby chuckled. "Goddammit, everybody worries too much. It's getting to where it ain't even no fun anymore being a nigger." He turned to see the kid's face somewhat astounded at that and he winked. "Now I've given you some good advice. Get Roxie and a bottle . . . she doesn't mind taking it slow unless it's a busy night . . . or go get a white girl, and forget the whole thing for a while."

Curtis got up and moved to the door.

Toby knew he wasn't about to follow his suggestions, but he'd had a good time making them. "Listen, Curtis, if you go in that bar, watch out for Nadine. She's that little one with the nice hips and the scar on her forehead. I hear she's got the clap." He laughed aloud and dipped his brush in the paint. When he turned, the kid was gone from the doorway.

Toby worked steadily, sipping from the bottle until it was nearly empty, just barely looking up as the people passed his doorway and spoke to him, sometimes briefly, sometimes at length. He kept his eyes on the signs and they had not begun to blur at all. He told Jelly Tatum that probably what was the matter with his hound dog was worms and the old lady from the grocery that she ought to see a doctor about her headaches if they came that regularly because it might be high blood and he'd loan her a little money if she needed it, but she said she could make it. And Nadine came in the shop wearing some kind of short pants that showed her belly button and had her white blouse tied up around under her brassiere, and he laughed when she got close and tried to make a red paint stripe across her bare stomach before she jumped back.

"I hear you got the clap," he said. "That'll give the bar a bad name."

"Who the fuck said that?" she asked, a little high on beer and ready for battle.

"Don't remember. Do you?"

"No, goddammit . . . I ain't got no clap."

"Really?"

Her teeth came flashing through the lips. "Well," she said, "maybe just a little."

He grinned. "You better get to the doctor and get a shot before you ruin all your trade."

"I'm gonna quit," she said.

"Good." He kept lettering steadily.

"The goddam amateurs ruin the business. They give it away."

"Seems unfair," he said, squinting as a passing car windshield caught the sunlight and flashed it in his eyes. "But you've got an advantage."

"What's that?"

"Well . . . you're a professional. You can do things they never thought of."

"That's right."

"But if you don't get cured, nobody will come within a mile of you."

"Yeah."

"You got money to quit for a while?"

She seemed suspicious of that question.

"If you got a little money, you better quit and get the cure. Then you are back in business."

"I got a little money."

"Okay."

"I know the sonbitch give it to me. If that fucker comes back I'll cut his nuts off."

"Do that and you sure do finish off a good customer."

He heard her giggle. "You bastard," she said.

He finished another sign. Not many more to go. His back was aching and the whiskey was almost gone. "Is Roxie in the bar?" he asked.

"No . . . she went upstairs with some trick. Guy with one leg."

He did not speak for a moment. "Is Levi down the street at the cab stand?"

He heard her move to the door to see. "He's sittin' there talkin' to somebody."

"When you go, do me a favor."

"Okay."

"Tell him to come over here when he gets a minute."

"Okay." She stepped out the door. In a voice that must have carried two blocks, alarming the police officer leaning against a telephone pole, she cried, "Hey, Levi . . . get your ass over here. Toby wants you."

He turned to the door, pained, but saw only a glimpse of her as she went down the sidewalk. He leaned back and lighted a cigarette. In a few moments Levi waddled into the shop.

"You want me, Toby?"

"Yeah . . . next fare you get," he withdrew his billfold and took out a five, "pick me up a fifth."

"Same thing?"

"Yeah . . ."

"You got it, Toby." The five disappeared and Levi was gone.

He knew what to do. It had been running through his mind since he left the doctor's office. He had argued with it, but there was always that long strip of paper and the doctor's voice . . . and he knew. He got off the stool and sat at his small desk. Turning the pages, licking his thumb carefully with each page, he found the number. He placed one finger under it and dialed. It rang four times and he was about to hang up, almost relieved, when the answer came. He swallowed a mouthful of spit and spoke in reply.

4

It was a quiet evening, not as muggy as it had been for a few days. Toby had cleaned up the trash that had collected in the corner of the room and swept, an activity that aroused Roxanne's suspicion that something was going on and it might have to do with another woman, which she would not like at all. Levi had peered in not long before, during a break from the cab when he went to his room and fixed a sandwich which he brought down to Toby's room and offered to share. And Levi noticed that all the clothes were put away and the place looked like maybe Toby had gone crazy and reverted back to the army days and was waiting for inspection.

He asked, "You havin' company?"

Toby sat on the made-up bed and nodded into the round, fat, black face.

"Who?"

"Just a man. Nothing big."

He didn't want to tell them about what the doctor had said, didn't want them to start a lot of nonsense because this was a thing he had to work on and already it was eight o'clock and he'd managed to get by with just a little over a pint, though he wasn't very steady. He thought about ol' Julius Bigger, who came in the shop nearly every day with his pitch, heading the other direction with all that goddam Panther stuff he'd been reading. He wanted the whole mothering world, wanted to go take Mississippi and Alabama and what else he didn't know to have a nigger country, and if some white man came down there acting smart-ass he'd better be out of town by sundown, just like it used to be for us in some places.

Levi leaned against the door and took another bite of the sandwich and scratched at his crotch while he chewed. Toby knew he could have talked to Levi if he had been a little drunk, but he didn't feel so good inside. He reached into the pocket of his clean shirt and withdrew a cigarette, struck a match and held it for a moment before seeking the tip of the cigarette. When he blew it out, he started to throw it on the floor until he remembered that he was having that man up there, so he put it in the ashtray which, for the first time in as long as anybody could remember, was empty.

"Toby."

He looked up and exhaled.

"You need a drink, Toby?"

The answer screamed in his mind but he ignored the honesty of the moment and shook his head.

"You don't seem very loose, Toby."

"I feel fine," he said slowly.

The sandwich was gone and Levi studied him there at the door, running that pink tongue around the teeth, cleaning up little bits of bread that had stuck in the spaces between his teeth. "I better get on the road."

Toby nodded.

Levi leaned away from the door and seemed to hesitate.

He looked at the dust on his shoes and said, "You want me to bring you a drink, Toby . . . for your company?"

"No, I'm fine."

Levi made a gesture with his hand and was gone from the doorway. In a few moments Toby heard his heavy steps moving down the stairs and then it was silent. He lay back on the bed and smoked a cigarette and thought that it was quite a crew they had living up there above those shops. All sharing the same bath except Roxanne, who had one of her own because in her business it was almost necessary.

He thought about Julius again. Ol' Julius was a lawyer and up until a couple of years ago he and the kid would have hit it off good, but he got to reading that literature and got mad when they killed those kids down at Orangeburg and had gone wild on the notion that somehow somebody was going to be able to convince the government of the United States to give half a dozen Southern states to the black people for a kind of nation . . . and had got so thoroughly involved with it that Toby couldn't understand why he didn't see how idiotic the whole thing was, why he didn't see that there wasn't the barest-assed chance that it would happen.

Although ol' Julius was a lawyer, he remembered when he worked in the fields and the sweat ran down his back in that little river between the muscles of his spine and he hit those weeds in that cotton field like he was severing the arteries of the white man who sent him out there. Somewhere along the line he'd finished high school, a black school that graduated him with a diploma worth maybe what the white kids had with an eighth-grade education, because the black teachers didn't know better than to say "they was," and he'd gone to a nigger college and worked his way through, serving food in the kitchen and sitting up all hours of the night trying to make it. And he did because in the nigger college they took about any warm body they could find then. After that—

mostly because he was black and maybe pretty good by that time—he got himself into the law school and made a success of it, for whatever that meant, because the money was with the white clients and he didn't have a prayer in hell to get them. So he took the black people, the ones from the bad houses, and he fought for them in city court and when they up and killed somebody and didn't have any money much to speak of, he went to the courthouse and tried to keep them out of jail, but with the white juries they were running, it was pretty hard. So he lived on what fees he could collect and he hated the white man a little more every time he lost a case, and probably for that reason he went from one extreme to another—the Kings and the Muslims and the Panthers. All the while nothing really changed very much, or fast, in this little South Carolina city, just gradually, and in the mood ol' Julius was in, maybe that wasn't enough.

Toby put out the cigarette and thought about Roxanne, but only for a moment because he heard her voice on the stairway and some deep-down tone and then the footsteps came along the hall and Roxie had this young boy from the junior college in tow and she squeezed his arm and said, "In there, baby, the next room. You go get ready and Roxie will be with you real soon."

The young man glanced a bit curiously as they passed Toby's door and went on down to Roxie's room. She came into Toby's room and closed the door. She was wearing a white blouse you could see through and a French brassiere underneath that showed all the cleavage in the world and a skirt that fairly hugged her ass and high heels that made her legs look nice, not quite yellow, like they said, though she owed that color to some white man's indiscretion, but light like the Lena Hornes of this world. She walked across his room, giving him a cheerful wave, and reached the door that separated her room from his. She ran her finger along the panel and caught the edge and swung it open to reveal the glass she'd had installed for him a long time ago. It was a mirror on her side, right along the bed so that if the guy wanted to watch himself make out he could, and on Toby's side it wasn't a mirror but a see-through thing like they had at supermarkets to discover if you were sticking a can of pork and beans inside your stocking when nobody was looking. Toby looked through the glass and saw the big young boy draping his shirt over the chair at the end of the bed and in a minute he dropped his trousers. Roxie stood there tapping her toe on the floor as she watched.

"I got me a live one, Toby," she said proudly. "I'm goin' for the record. You gonna time me?"

"Yes," he said softly, somewhat in wonder.

The boy removed his shorts and already he was prepared.

"God knows if I don't get in there, that thing will blow without me touching him. Okay, baby," she said, going to the door, "I'll signal with my hand and you count the seconds."

Toby twisted around so that he could see the signal and, taking off his wristwatch, saw her enter the room and go over to the black boy and snuggle up close. She took his hand and put it on her breast and let her eyes drop to see what effect that was having, which was considerable. Then she began to tease him at the genitals as she kicked one shoe free, then the other. She was out of the blouse in a moment, like she didn't take it off but it just disappeared, and flipped the bra free and shook her shoulders and rubbed it all against his bare chest and he grinned like an idiot and then she let him pull the zipper to the skirt and she stepped out of it, just letting it fall to the floor, and he saw that that was all, no slip, no nothing underneath, and he must have thought about sitting next to her in the bar, not knowing all that time that it was right there ready. She took his hand and led it to her business and carefully took his finger and put it there and he grinned some more and she knew she had that poor dum-dum ready and there wasn't no need to dally. So she scurried away from him and hit the bed, throwing her arms back over her head, running her hands through her long black hair, and here he came. She flopped those legs into position and took him and guided him. And when she had him ready, she raised her hand up in the air, the signal, and started letting out animal sounds and gyrating all over the bed, slamming it to that poor nigger boy so wildly he didn't know what hit him.

Toby watched the second hand move sluggishly around the face of the watch, glancing up to see the boy hanging on for dear life while she made that thing snap and squeeze and gyrate in every believable direction. His face got a kind of surprised expression on it and then she popped him good and his eyes closed as the spasm did that miraculous thing in his brain that makes human life continue successfully. He had no sooner gone limp than she cocked one leg against the mattress and tossed him like a child over on his back, the black organ falling free, still erect, and she got up and stood on the floor and looked into the mirror and winked. Toby looked down at the second hand and marked the time it had taken. And then, knowing that Toby had done his job, Roxanne climbed back in the bed with the young man and ran her fingers along his back and, though Toby couldn't hear, was surely telling him that she'd go for him again for another ten or fifteen, if he had it, and she'd play with him real good if he liked and take a long time. But he'd had his shot and he either didn't have ten dollars or he'd sure got his money's worth because he shook his head. She took his hand and pulled him gently from the bed to the sink where she took his organ, going limp now, in her hand and washed him carefully and then put some alcohol on it, c〜 and refreshing, and wiped him dry and clean. She went over to the chair and took his shorts and his trousers and handed them to him, caressing him just a bit, and found the skirt on the floor and drew it over her hips, then the brassiere and blouse, and before he had his trousers on she slipped into her high heels and came up and kissed him on the neck and said something softly and the young man grinned and slapped her, a little self-consciously, on the buttocks and with the ten dollars in her purse she sat on the bed and lighted a cigarette while he finished dressing. Soon he went to the door and she was jiggling her leg furiously with anticipation as he left the room. Toby heard his footsteps go along the hall and down the stairs but before the sounds had ceased Roxie jerked to her feet and in an instant his door was thrown open and she stood spread-legged and full of excitement and asked, "Did I break my record?"

Toby moistened his lips, wishing he could please her, wishing that for the sole glory of a black prostitute he could lie and give her a kind of unique gift, but she depended on him to be honest and it wasn't any good unless the whole thing was straight and fair.

"You missed by ten seconds, Roxie. It was that close."

Her face showed the disappointment because this had really been a likely prospect. "Well, shit," she said. Then as though she had not already expressed the disappointment, she repeated, "Shit."

"Sweetpot . . ." Toby said, "the record is, I suppose, maybe a world's record, and if you remember correctly it was a white boy seventeen years old and probably his first piece and even if it had been a black boy, all things being the same, there wasn't that erotic aspect of sleeping with a twenty-four-year-old black woman . . . so it may be a while before you break that record . . . though, dear, it was a terrific performance."

"Shit," she said again. Then, as though it no longer mattered, very suddenly the effect such anticipation had had was forgotten and she relaxed and came over to the bed where he lay and sat beside him. "Toby, you're sober."

He smiled and let his hand fall on her arm.

"Your friend . . ." and she said it in a strange way, a suspicious way, "will be here pretty soon?"

"Yes."

He saw that tongue trace a neat line around the edge of her lip and knew she wanted to ask about it but would not, though it had her worried, the idea that it might be a woman. He tightened his touch on her arm.

"Roxie . . . it's kind of a business deal."

Her dark eyes cut to him and there was a hint of fire there. "I'm in business." Like maybe that was what he was doing, sleeping with some black woman—which she knew goddam well he did once in a while, though not on a regular basis like with her.

"No, baby . . . it's not that."

And suddenly her mouth swept into a smile, like she had never been worried about it, and she said, "Honey, I never thought that at all."

He felt the laughter coming out of his gut and it slipped nicely, smoothly to his throat and when he laughed she caught the infection of it and giggled with him, her eyes crinkling up so beautifully, and it all died slowly so that she leaned over and nuzzled her body against his and kissed his neck. While she did that he thought about how five minutes before she knew he was watching her throw all she had into sexual intercourse with a man she would not see again perhaps, or at least not often, and how that didn't matter to her at all because it didn't mean anything . . . because she always came back, came to Toby, who was forty-three and didn't make it like those young studs, and she cuddled up against him and he knew that in some way, some incredible process in the brain, she loved him. As she lay against him so sincerely, with the sperm of another man not yet flushed from her body, he wanted to tell her, wanted to hold her to him and say that he was going to die unless . . . or maybe even . . . but then almost a sob came to his throat, partly because he was so sober at this hour and needed a drink so badly and partly because he knew that, with Roxie as with all of them, it was long ago established that he was the sponge into whose soul they dripped their sadness and remorse and hatred and . . . the all of it. He knew if he told her, she would worry and instead of coming to him with all that sad jazz, all that need, she'd start trying to comfort him, but she didn't know quite what to do and her world would fall apart . . . and so he kept silent and felt her body next to his and closed his eyes, thinking of the taste of liquor going down his throat and wishing he had some other kind of choice to make.

He let his arm slip around her slim waist and wondered at a twenty-four-year-old woman needing a man who was so close to ruin and needing him so badly. He could feel her breathing becoming steady and knew that she was napping, that she was going to sleep for a time against his shoulder, content that he wasn't seeing another woman, though she had just asked him to watch her performance and she saw no incongruity in that at all.

And he told himself that he shouldn't either because that was what she was. More than a dozen times, God knows how many, she had hinted that if he would take her and live with her she would never turn another trick, and he believed her but he'd never been able to do that, though he couldn't really understand the sense that told him no, the knowledge that it would not be right that came from somewhere inside him. He felt her head heavy on his shoulder and she made little sounds in her throat as she slept and he thought that there was more to love . . . actually that there was something called love, a need, a greater need than the satisfaction of the loins and that was what he provided for her, for whatever reason, and that was what the kid came for, to talk all those terrible long hours about the black man and the white man and how they had to make it together . . . and old Levi bringing him liquor just so Toby could drink and listen while he talked about almost anything. God love Levi who at least had cool and maybe loved him honestly, more than any of the others, because Levi didn't ask for much. Roxie had told him once, no, not once, over a period of time how her old man, her father, had come into the room while she'd been napping and her mother was off at the McLendons doing maid work and there was nobody in the house and she was fifteen and he knew goddam well that she wasn't his daughter because of the color and maybe it was because of that that he felt that way, or maybe it was because he would have done it anyway, and he came in just as calm as could be, with three good slugs of moonshine in his gut, and he closed the door and zipped that fly and she looked up and knew what was happening and knew there wasn't a goddam thing in the world she could do. He came over and threw her skirt up and looked down at her like if she made a sound he'd hit her in the mouth so hard her head would ache for a week. She was terrified, and just as casually as hell he took his time taking off his trousers, looking down at her steadily, hating her maybe for what some white man had done to his wife, and this somehow was his revenge, as though he had waited until her body was ready, until the pubic hair had come and her blood came once a month and she was what amounted to a woman. Then he came over to the bed and, standing over her, said for her to take off her pants. She told Toby that she had looked at the distance to the door but that he was between

them and she didn't have a prayer, and with a gut full of that
white liquor he'd have beat her half to death if she tried. All
the other kids in the family were good and black and she
knew he was thinking this as he stood there with his organ
all ready, which she saw was pretty formidable though she'd
seen only a couple at the age of fifteen. And so she slipped
her thumbs inside the panties and pulled them down and the
old man . . . not old really, maybe forty by then . . . watched
without smiling because he'd waited a long time for this day
to get even with whatever white man his woman had slept
with and made his daughter the color she was. Then he came
down on her, ripping away at her brassiere, and plunged
that thing in her to the hilt and it hurt like God wouldn't believe, and then he got it all the way and began to say crazy
things about her mother and every time he said something,
he'd slam it to her. She begged Toby to understand and he
did, or at least tried to. The old man gave her the full shot
and when he was done he rolled over and took a hard hand
and turned her face to him and looked at her for a long time.

In a little while he got up and put on his clothes and told
her if she said a word he'd kill her, which she believed to be
true. He came back four more times before she left. She took
her little canvas bag and, while he was drunk, slipped out of
the house with ten dollars she had stolen from the hiding
place. She got a bus north, but only about five dollars' worth
of ride, which left her standing on a hot street in Yorksboro.
She found a room and lit out making all the restaurants,
asking for work in a kitchen. And she was lucky because that
guy she found didn't care whether she was fifteen or fifty as
long as she'd take sixty cents an hour and keep moving.

That's the way it had been, she told him, for a couple of
years, and she lived with the fear that one day her old man
would find her, but he never did, maybe never tried because
she figured later her mother would suffer silently for a while

and one night she just might take a knife and cut his head
off while he slept, for what he did. But she had enough to eat
from the restaurant and managed to make it and didn't see
much of men. Until she was past seventeen and this stud got
to looking at her as she walked to where she lived. One day,
as she passed him, he just eased out to the cracked sidewalk
and put his hand on her arm and said he'd give her ten dollars for it. She pulled her arm free and didn't even answer
but she did think about it, how she had to work like the Lord
wouldn't believe for sixty cents an hour and that would be a
pretty fast ten. The stud was there the next day, sitting on his
porch, but his woman was next to him and he just craned his
neck and looked up at the clouds as she walked by.

But one day he was alone again and as she passed he am-
bled out there and she looked at him for a long moment and
then got a little smile to her mouth and said, "Come on."

He followed her down the street and she went into her
room and closed the door and began to take off her clothes.
But she wasn't stupid. She showed him her breasts, which
were pretty fabulous by then, and she said, holding out her
hand, "Ten."

He dug out a billfold and counted out the money, which
she took, folded, and snapped in her purse. She said she was
lucky that first time because he didn't want anything unusual, just a straight date, and he was easy with her and she
didn't know enough to realize that she wasn't supposed to
really go with him, really get a bang out of it. Maybe because
he took his time and maybe because she was a born hooker,
she got that good feeling. When he left, she lay there and
stared at the ceiling and knew she'd found her place. But it
wasn't all that simple . . . when she turned pro, which she
could do because of what she had for a body and the color
she was, she found it wasn't all that simple. She got herself
a pimp and he beat the peewaddledy shit out of her some-

times, it seemed, just for the hell of it. Since she didn't care much for that jazz, she got away from him and when he came after her she stood in the doorway with a butcher knife and waited, hardly breathing, until he saw murder in her eyes and backed off, and after that she gave those fancy-dressed boys a wide berth. But there were the weird ones, the ones who didn't want it straight, and she found that a little hard to take. She found Levi Duvall one night in a bar and he said there was a bunch of white cats who liked it dark and, if she'd give him a little cut, he'd steer them to her. She moved up above the sign shop because Levi lived there and that's when she met Toby. How that got going he didn't know, because he'd never said a word about it to her, but when she wasn't busy she'd drop down there to his shop and watch him letter, sometimes by the hour, never saying a word, fascinated by the way he turned a brush in his fingers as he made a stroke. Until that night he was lying on his bed reading and she rapped on his door. He took a drink from his glass and said come in . . . and she just opened the door and closed it behind her and took off her robe and took the book out of his hands, turning it over face down so she didn't lose his place, and snuggled up to him.

He said, "Roxanne."

"Ummmmhum."

"I don't have any money."

She reached up and put her hands over his lips—her answer.

She didn't pull any fancy tricks, didn't try to show off what she had learned. It was like the other was work and this was something else. This was born out of some other need. That was the way it started.

Now, he touched her shoulder, let his hand rest on the light flesh. "Roxie."

She opened her eyes and sighed before turning her head.

"My friend will be here soon."

"Okay." She stretched and eased her legs over the side of the bed and sat with her shoulders slumped for a moment. "I'm goin' down to get a beer. You want me to bring some back?" she asked.

"No."

He looked at the back of her head and she moved just a bit and he knew she was trying to figure it out. "Okay," she said and went to the door. "See you later, baby."

He heard her feet on the floor in her room. She closed the door and he went to the panel and opened it. He watched as she put on a dress and dabbed a little perfume about her ears. She came to the mirror and looked at herself and it was as though she were looking directly at him and he wondered if she knew he was watching. Roxie smiled at her image or maybe at him—he couldn't be sure. She turned and went to the door as he closed the panel, passing his room quickly. His legs were trembling. He needed a drink something awful.

5

The man came about eight while there was still a little light in the sky. Toby didn't know if he'd shake hands or not, but he did. He was tall, thin, with a couple of blue lines in the veins of his cheeks, and Toby knew, without his saying a word, he'd been through it. He had a book in his hand.

"Toby, isn't it?" he asked.

"Yes," Toby said. "Come in."

"My name's Bill."

Toby pulled the straight-back chair over near the bed and Bill sat on it and glanced around the shabby room. Not much showed in his face.

"You've got a problem?"

Toby nodded. He didn't know what he was supposed to do.

Bill smiled and leaned back, putting the book on the bed next to Toby. "How much have you had today?"

"About a pint. Mostly this morning."

"You feel bad?"

"Shaky."

Bill nodded. He had a good tan, like he either worked outside or played golf. "Can you read, Toby?"

Something caught in his throat and he had to hesitate before he answered because he knew he probably had a better education than this white man. But the man was not there to do anything but try to help him. Maybe he had run into this before and it was just something he had to know. "Yes. I can read," Toby said slowly.

"I want you to read this book. It's a good book. It explains the whole thing. But the most important thing is . . . you've got to have a sincere desire . . . unless you've got that, you'll just have to ride it out until you do."

He didn't know exactly why he said it—he hadn't meant to—but he sensed a great relief that there was somebody, anybody, even a white man he could say it to. "I don't have much liver left. And I've got a bad heart. The doctor said I didn't have a choice if I wanted to be around."

"All right, Toby." The voice was gentle.

"I don't know if I have that desire. Sometimes it seems hopeless, like I might as well just drown in it."

"Yes . . . I know." They said nothing for a few moments. Bill leaned forward slightly and met Toby's eyes. "Do you need to go to the hospital?"

Toby shook his head.

"Read the book. You've only got to worry about today. That's important. We all have to learn that. All you've got is today, and a man can make it one day. If tomorrow comes, you work on that one, but you don't think about it until it gets here. Do you understand that?"

Toby nodded.

"You've got my number."

"Yes."

Bill stood. "Before you take a drink tomorrow, call me. I own a little business, but I can leave for a while. I'll come talk to you. If you take a drink first, don't call me. It wouldn't do any good."

Toby nodded and let his eyes move to the book.

"Read that, Toby. When you finish, give me a call."

Toby agreed.

Bill went toward the door and, when he turned, something painful was in his face, as though he was ashamed of what he had to say. "It takes two to have a meeting, Toby. I'm your man. We have meetings upstairs over the Coca Cola plant on Tuesday nights but, Toby, we aren't perfect and we've never had a . . ." He licked his lips and looked down.

Toby gave him the word he had not been able to use. "A nigger," he said softly and smiled slightly.

Bill moistened his lips again. "Well . . . we hoped we could get a black group started. You're welcome as far as I'm concerned . . ."

"No . . . I understand."

"I'll come here. It just takes two people, Toby."

"Yes, I understand."

"I don't think that other is important . . . all that matters is that you make one day. And call me if you need me."

"Yes."

The white man was finally able to meet his eyes again. "Take it easy," he said. He made a motion with his hand and went to the door.

"Thank you," Toby said.

Then he was gone. Toby took the book in his hand but he did not open it. He kept thinking that he was not going to be able to sleep, that there wasn't any way for him to sleep, even with the pills, unless he had a few drinks . . . that it would go on for maybe a week or more before he could sleep again. But the man said the way it worked was you didn't think about a week . . . just today.

He put the book in the fruit box and sat down. Sometimes the doctors just told a man that about his liver and maybe about his heart. They knew he had a problem and they just

said it to scare a man into doing something about it. His liver
might be as sound as . . .

He heard Levi coming, knew by his sound. Levi came into
the room; his round face cracked into a three-dollar smile. He
slapped his sagging belly. "Had me some fresh greens. Cornbread. Boy, they was good. What you doin', Toby?"

"Just taking it easy," Toby said, remembering.

"Yeah . . . you want to go ride in the cab for a while?"

"No . . . I thought I'd read some."

"It's a nice evenin'."

"Yes." And it was going to be a long, terrible night. And
other nights.

"Well, I guess I'll go run a couple fares."

Toby drew a deep breath and listened to his own words
come drifting back at him. "Levi, there's some money in the
fruit box there. Pick me up a pint and drop it by."

Levi went to the box and counted out the bills. "I'll just
get it right now, Toby."

"Yes, that would be good. Thanks, Levi."

Levi crushed the bills in his fist and took off down the hallway. Toby lay back and stared at the ceiling. He wouldn't
drink it; he'd just have it there in case he got to feeling bad.
He wouldn't break the seal.

He thought it was Levi coming back at first, but there
were two of them and he saw Roxie pass his doorway with a
white man, and she did not look his way. He heard her door
close and lay there looking at the ceiling and hearing her
voice, gay and tinkly, until after a few minutes it got quiet
except for some of those subtle sounds, and he wished Levi
would hustle a bit, though he reminded himself he wasn't going to snap that cap . . . just have it around in case he got
sick.

He lay with his hands at his sides, trying to make them
loose. How in the name of God does a man live one day at a

time? It sounded so simple, but there was always the rent and liquor . . . even that white liquor he had to drink when he got caught short, and there were no signs to paint . . . and something to eat and you had to hustle like all get out to make it, and if you were a nigger you had to hustle that much more . . . but he didn't have to worry about buying the liquor anymore. Maybe that would make a difference. Maybe if he got a few days behind him, it would get easier.

Hell, Levi probably got some fare that took him way out in the city and he hadn't had a chance to pick up the pint. It didn't matter.

Then his mind drifted back and he started wondering where Sal went. He'd wondered that for so many years and so hopelessly that he couldn't remember all the times. She never even hinted that something was going on. He hadn't suspected. What a damned fool he must have been. Danny was four . . . no, maybe he was five, and he would be going to school pretty soon and already Toby was buying him those little kid books and showing him the letters, the words under the pictures of giraffes and elephants . . . and Sal would sit across the room listening to the radio and he thought it was all good because he didn't go out at night, just stayed home with them and sipped a little whiskey until it got time to go to bed and when it got late, he'd take Danny to his bed and hold him close for a while. He came home that day, a pint in his pocket, and walked in and found the note on the screen door. He didn't really believe it, thought it was something of a joke, for God's sake, until he looked in the closet and saw that her clothes were all gone, the dresser drawers empty. He opened the bottle and took a good one and sat down and kept asking himself *why in the hell? why?* and he just sat on the edge of the bed and drank that pint. She'd left Danny at a neighbor's down the street, the note said. When he finished the pint he was still sober and he got up and went to the neighbor's and took Danny's hand and led him home. They had given him his dinner and he asked Toby where his mother was and Toby said she'd gone on a visit. He got out Danny's pajamas and dressed him and managed to get him in bed, but when he held him close like he always did a sob came from down deep inside and he had to get out of there fast, and he made it to the other bedroom and closed the door.

For a long time after that he thought she'd get it out of her system, that one day she'd come back, and it took a couple of years for him to know . . . no, not *know* but feel that Sal was gone and, wherever she was, whoever took her away, they were making it and that was it. She was gone. So he got to working hard and making some money, sticking some aside for Danny's college, and he would come home and check over Danny's school papers and drink a pint or so.

He heard a door open and Roxanne murmuring something softly and in a minute the white man went down the hall hurriedly. Roxie closed her door.

Danny was smart, almost at the top of his class, and he'd turned into a handsome boy. He didn't do much running around, not wild like some of them. He'd come in and do his homework, and then he'd sit down with Toby and they'd have a drink before Danny went to bed. Once he got it bad for a girl and Toby had a hard talk with him about using precaution, reminding him that if he got himself a kid he'd lose his chance at college and it wasn't worth the difference going in bare. And Danny said, yes, he understood. He didn't suspect that Danny would enlist. He had it all planned that in the fall he'd go to college, but Danny came in that night and said, "Pops, we got to talk." Toby knew by the way his son looked at him that it was important, so he poured them a drink and they sat down. Danny was ignoring his drink and rubbing his hands together. "I joined up today, Pops," he said.

Toby frowned . . . he remembered that he had been anticipating Danny's announcement that he wanted to get married, and he was ready for that, but he couldn't seem to get this straight in his head. "Danny . . . what the hell?"

The boy looked him in the eye. "The man said if I serve, they'll give me the G.I. Bill. Then, with what you got for me and what I can save, I can go to school."

"You've done it . . . already?"

"Yes."

He took a long pull from the glass, remembering a few visions that he had never shared with anyone, not even Danny. One of them was withdrawing a bayonet from a man's chest. It got stuck in there and the man was looking at him with his mouth open in shock and he had to put his foot against the man's body and pull to get it out, and then the man, still looking at him, went down and was able to put his hand to the wound while his mouth worked soundlessly. Then something else moved nearby and he cut for the brush and didn't see the man anymore, but that instant, that vision, that feel was going to be with him the rest of his life. There were others, but that one was the worst.

"Can you stop it now?" Toby asked softly.

"I don't want to, Pops . . . I want to go."

Toby ran his hand across his face roughly. "What did you join, son?"

"The army."

"Did they say anything about school? You got a fine record, Danny. Maybe they'll send you to school."

"Maybe."

Toby looked at the floor.

"Pops . . . don't be mad with me."

"No . . . no . . ." He thought he was going to choke up, so

he waited until that feeling passed. "No, I just wanted you to go to college. Ever since . . ." And Sal came to his mind and he had to stop again. "I just wanted you to go to college and . . . maybe law or . . ."

"Pops, I'll do that. Don't you see . . . when I get back, I'll have that bill to help me and if I save . . ."

Toby nodded. He took another drink and looked his son squarely in the eye and said very slowly. "Listen, son . . ." Danny listened. "Don't be a fool. Whatever happens, don't be a fool and don't be reckless. You understand?"

Danny nodded but he didn't know that vision of the man with a bayonet stuck in his chest, so he couldn't have really understood.

Toby went to the train station with him and made it all right with a good pint in his belly. It wasn't until after he had left that it got him, and he made it home . . . and for the second time in his life he put his face into that pillow. There was a third time. The white man talked about days . . . *one day* . . . well, that was one day. Not the day he got the notice but later when they came and he had to admit they did it with a lot of dignity . . . they did right by that black boy, the army did. They gave him the flag and he didn't know much about that war—it wasn't the kind he'd known. People didn't feel the same about this one. But he took the flag under his arm and, like he was an old, old man, the sergeant placed his hand under his elbow and helped him into the limousine and he made it fine with a pint in his belly. He went home and put the flag on the dresser in the bedroom and fell over that bed. It came up out of him and it was hideous. When it was over, he got drunk and sat in the darkness, smoking, and wished he knew where Sal was, wished he could sit down with her, no matter where she'd gone or who the man was, and just have a talk, tell her what a fine boy he'd been, how he'd studied and was going to college when he got back and maybe study law or . . .

Levi came up the stairway. He knew it was Levi by his walk, kind of heavy and slow.

"Hey, Toby, here's your bottle."

He did not turn. He felt the weight added to the bed. "Thanks, Levi," he said.

"How come you're in the dark? You want a light on?"

"No . . . not right now."

"Well . . . there's a good show on the T.V. You want to come down and watch?"

"Not right now, Levi. I'll be down later."

"Okay, honey . . . come on down."

Levi hurried down the hallway to see the program. Toby felt the weight against his side. He wasn't going to drink it. He wasn't going to pop the seal. It was just to have there. Because he had the desire the white man had talked about and it didn't matter if they didn't much want him to go to the meetings . . . it only took two and the white man said call him anytime. He'd leave his business and come. That was pretty good. They had to have something. Then he just closed his eyes for a moment and shook his head on the pillow.

He let his hand slip over there and he felt the bottle. Sometimes they just tell you about the liver to scare you. He hadn't ever seen any spiders coming out of the goddam walls. None of that crazy stuff. They try to scare you because they think that's the thing to do.

He snapped the seal and pulled himself up so he wouldn't spill it and felt the smooth glass against his lips. And it went down easy until he could feel the nerves start to get quiet . . . three swallows. He put the cap back on the bottle and lay back, waiting for the effect. When it came, he took another drink and got up, putting the bottle in his rear pocket. He went down the stairs, feeling in his pocket for his keys, and opened the door to the shop. He turned on the light and put the bottle on the table.

Roxanne came in behind him and sat on a chair while he mixed the paint. "Hey, baby, you all right?" she asked.

"Sweetpot," he said, "I'm fine. How's your black ass?"

"It's just sweet as pie . . . ready for lovin'."

"Well, now we just maybe better 'tend to that after a while," he said.

"Sugar, let's just do that."

He sat before the painting of the black doll and looked at the mouth for a long while. He wanted some lines, subtle ones, about the mouth. He waited a long time before he took the brush and dabbed it in the paint.

She said, "Toby, baby, why do you paint such sad pictures?"

He didn't answer her. He kept looking at the mouth of the black doll. Then he said, "Not all sad, Roxie. Not all happy . . . just like it is."

She did not reply because this was beyond her. She didn't know what he meant but he knew that she understood it was important to him. He looked at the doll with the brush poised in his hand. He was steady now but he was afraid to touch the paint to the canvas. It had to be just right. So he waited, staring into the face. Nobody knew . . . there was nobody anymore who knew. But Toby did and he thought about the boy, when he was five . . . and now he was getting a little drunk, not much, and he saw in that doll's face so many things . . . the pictures of elephants and giraffes . . .

"Roxanne."

"Yeah, baby."

"Pour me a drink in that glass, will you?"

"Yeah, sugar."

And he sat holding the brush but he did not touch the

painting. He wanted the face to be sad, but the face was not entirely sad and maybe he had it right. The face had never been very sad and he hadn't been able to look into the box with the flag because they wouldn't let him. He took the glass without looking back at Roxanne and took it all in one swallow.

"Roxanne," he said again.

"Yeah."

"Maybe it's finished. Maybe I've done all I can."

"Honey," she said, "it's just fine. Real fine."

He put the wet brush on the table. It would be hard and stiff in the morning, but it didn't matter. He would bring it back to life tomorrow. "You through for the night?" he asked.

"Yeah . . . waitin' for you."

"Okay."

He stood and turned out the light. She waited beside him, close to him, as he locked the door. He put his arm around her twenty-four-year-old waist and led her to the stairs. He felt every step beneath his feet as he trudged up the stairs.

"Sweetpot . . ."

She liked it when he said that. When he said that he was the real Toby. "Yeah, baby."

"I feel pretty good." He could feel the bottle weighing on his back pocket.

"We gonna have us a good time, Toby."

"Yes, we are."

They reached the top of the stairs. He led her to the room and she started undressing. He took out the bottle and took another good drink, leaving only one more good one or two small ones. He smiled and she came to him and put her arms around his neck.

"Toby."

"Yeah, sweetpot."

"Toby, I love you."

He put his hands on her breasts because that was what she wanted him to do and wondered if she had any idea how much he needed her to say that.

6

Roxanne lay nude on the bed in the velvet darkness, feeling the breeze from the window fan, listening to the hum, the slight rattle where the metal vibrated against the window sill, watching the glimmers of light that managed to creep through the window, reflections from headlights of passing cars almost rhythmic in procession. Toby had made good music. He had turned her every way possible and with that liquor in him he had all the time in the world, stopping after she had gasped the first time and reaching for the bottle and taking a little drink, still with her, and lighting a cigarette in the darkness, passing it to her as they traded jags, talking softly until the red glow became warm to their fingers, at which time he casually tossed it out the window into the alley and started all over again. It was so much she thought she was going to cry, not from the sensation—she knew that only too well—but from the feeling of belonging, being Toby's woman . . . and when he touched her it was like she figured God had meant it to be. She had considered, really ached not to *do* anything to prevent taking his child inside her, because the way it was, Toby wouldn't let her move in, would never, not ever go over there where she had the fan, where it was cooler, because that's where she made her money . . . but if she could take his child in her, she was afraid he would find out and maybe she'd be so . . . happy that she'd have to tell him, or maybe he'd know somehow, like he always seemed to know things you didn't have to say, and he'd sure as God go downstairs and pack his brushes in a box and fill a cardboard suitcase with his clothes and get on the next bus to someplace . . . so she didn't do that to him. She did have the courage to ask him one night. They were lying side by side, resting, and she ran her fingers along his face like the blind feeling the features of someone else, and she almost whispered, "Toby . . . I want a baby."

He did not turn but she felt a change in the muscles under her fingers.

"You know. I want *your* baby."

His voice was very deep, almost inaudible. "No," he said.

She lay beside him for a while, not speaking. It was because she was selling herself. She understood then. "I'd quit. If I could have a baby, I'd quit. I'd never do it again, Toby. I'd be a good mother. You wouldn't have to take me in or even give me money."

He was silent.

"Toby?"

"Yes."

"Would you do that?"

"No." Softly.

Her fingers tightened against his cheek. She felt her nails against the flesh and an anger welled in her and it was all she could do to keep from cutting into the flesh, and then it passed and she was deflated. "Why? What would it hurt you?"

He took her hand from his face firmly and put it on the

bed between them. He withdrew. "I've had a child. A son,"
he said, and the sound was no sound she had ever heard
from him. Not angry . . . not anything she could understand.
"He died," Toby said.

"A baby?"

"No . . . a *man*." Something happened to his voice.

They lay together for a long while and she did not ask
anymore, but later she thought that he wouldn't have to
know. She could fake him and by the time she started showing the child, maybe he'd change his mind . . . but she knew,
even as she entertained that fantasy, that he would not
change and somehow he would know. He wouldn't marry
her, which didn't matter. It would be enough if she could
move into the room or if they could get a little place or
maybe unscrew the screws that held the door between the
rooms and open it into two rooms. She could fix it up nice
and he could share her bath and not have to go down the
hall with that bunch, sometimes to wait in line, because Levi
took forever to have a movement. But he wouldn't do that
either. She had tried that so goddam many times he started
laughing and shaking his head when she brought up the
subject, no matter how cleverly she tried to ease into the
matter. Sometimes it got her good and mad, the bastard,
and occasionally she'd slam the door, especially when she'd
had a good week, and she'd go to Charlotte and swing with
those cats, those sharp cool ones who were on the pills and
the pot, and she'd get a bellyful of it, all the time knowing
that Toby was back there, knowing what she was doing and
not saying a word, not storming up there to find her and
jerk her arm out of socket to get her back where she belonged . . . oh, God, where she belonged. He'd be sitting at
that easel laboring over those goddam signs by the hour
and sipping a little whiskey along, not too sure she'd come
back but maybe figuring, at least not surprised when she

appeared at the door of his room later and leaned against it and looked at him for a long time, hoping he'd be mad or turn his back on her so she could get a signal . . . but no, he'd just lie there looking at her, not smiling, not much of anything. She'd walk across the room—she could see herself doing it—saucy as a bitch in heat, and sit on his bed.

"I been to Charlotte," she'd say. "I had me a good time."

He would nod. "I noticed you were gone," he'd say, say it exactly right, like it mattered, but if that's what she wanted to do, all right. *All right.* And those black eyes would be staring at her through those idiotic GI type gold frames, like he'd never look away, didn't need to look away because he hadn't done anything to look away about. Then she'd lower her lashes and feel her hands turning into tight little knobs and the muscles in her jaw would tighten and she would say, "I got mad at you."

He would put his hand on hers, lightly. "I know, sweet-pot," he'd say.

And that goddam silly word would plain slide like warm butter right over her body and she would just start leaning in his direction, her body stiff, so near to crying she didn't know what held it back, coming to rest against him on the bed, snuggling her head against him and lying for a long time that way.

A couple of times she had caught him—not many because he didn't go often—but once in a while something came over Toby and he'd go down to one of those bad houses where they had all that gambling and drinking and nigger bitches who went around half-naked, taking the boys upstairs and giving them the clap for nothing. He'd be gone maybe a day, sometimes just overnight, and he'd come back, never say a word to her . . . he'd never say a word but she knew her way around and she *got* the word. That one time she came in and slammed the goddam door of his shop where he was working on a sign and he looked up at her like a saint, like he hadn't been out screwing the juice out of some nigger bitch.

"Where the hell you been?" she had demanded.

And that right hand just kept on dipping into the paint and smoothing it on and the finesse with that brush somehow reminded her how he might have touched one of those women, like he had touched her so often and so effectively.

"You answer me, goddammit," she said and it came from somewhere deep in her throat like an animal. She reached the easel and jerked the sign away and tore it into maybe ten pieces and threw them on the floor and stamped her feet on them in a rage. And Toby just sat there for an instant before he leaned over and picked up his bottle and took a drink, just a little one, and slowly screwed the cap back on and put it down on the floor very carefully. Then he lifted his head from the torn sign and, like maybe a school teacher to a child, shook his head slowly, side to side, and his eyes were hard and she knew then that she had to back off or that was the goddam ballgame.

A couple of times she had figured to hell with him, but there was always that persistent voice beneath the rage and that voice told her the God's truth, that if she went too far, if she ripped it good, Toby would be gone and when Toby was gone for a little while he seemed gone a long time, and if he was *really* gone, he would be gone forever. So that time she took a clean cardboard and placed it back on the easel, her hands shaking terribly, and turned around and walked out, leaving the door open like he had it, and went down to the Red Dot store and bought a big bottle of gin and told Levi to keep any son of a bitch who wanted to fuck the hell out of there because she wasn't fucking nobody today. She got drunk. She got so blind drunk, which she couldn't do worth a damn, that after a while the ceiling got to going around and her belly turned upside down and the next thing she knew she was crawling through her own vomit to the commode, hanging on for dear life with the dry heaves, and that time somebody told him she must be dying up there because he came up and, although she couldn't see him hardly at all, she knew it was him and he lifted her up and washed her off and took her to bed on her stomach because he said you don't get so sick that way. When she got up, the place didn't smell good but all the mess was gone, as well, by God, as what was left in the bottle, which he sure as hell took and drank.

But she was his woman. Everybody knew that up and down the street. None of those studs ever bothered her anymore, trying for that free stuff, because they knew she belonged to Toby and that to even buy her a beer in the bar was throwing money down a rat hole; they'd get nothing unless they slapped the money in her palm first.

Toby wasn't going to change. He wouldn't even let her stay in his room all night, except that one time. The white man had sent Levi up there while he waited in the cab. Some pathologist—whatever that was—from Chicago maybe and he said he wanted something special but he'd pay good, and when Roxie asked Levi how good, he said a hundred dollars, which was like a live one for sure. The man was about fifty, a nice-looking man, no paunch, sober, dressed up nice like a professor. He came into the room and looked at her for a minute and then, maybe satisfied, tossed a paper sack on the bed.

"Levi said you wanted something special." There wasn't much she wouldn't do anymore, if they had the money, but a hundred dollars was a whole hell of a lot of money and either he was stupid or he wanted something crazy. He did.

He counted out the bills, five twenties, and put them on the table. She moved closer to him and let her robe slip open so he could see her breasts and she could tell by his face that he agreed she had a fabulous body and that he liked her color very much.

His voice was gentle, kind. "You'll find some rope in the bag. I want you to take the pieces and tie my hands very tightly behind my back. Then I want you to tie my ankles together."

She did not know what to expect next. Weirdos, she'd had, but nothing like this before.

"Then take the adhesive tape and run it around my hands and ankles also to make sure I'm bound securely."

"Yeah."

"In the bag you will find a razor blade, several large pins, and some towels."

She must have looked very wary.

"Don't worry . . . you'll come to no harm, I promise you."

"What do you want me to do, man?"

"Cut with the razor blade. Jab with the pins. Cut above my elbows, mostly on the back and stomach, whatever way I turn. Just short gashes. Nothing deep. The pins are large so that you may grip them in your fist. Leave about a quarter of an inch exposed below your fist and hit me with the point. Then tear the pin away, making a long scratch, but always above the line where a short-sleeved shirt might show the wounds."

She shook her head. "I don't know. I just don't know."

"I will make sounds. If I scream, would it be heard?"

"It might."

"Then you can cover my mouth with adhesive tape. I will still make sounds, but they won't be alarming."

It seemed incredible that the man meant what he was saying. So cool. "I don't know," she said again, like maybe she wanted something in writing, but this was no ordinary john and he wasn't about to put something in writing because that would leave him naked.

"Please," he said. "I'm from out of town. I've come to Charlotte on a professional trip. I drove down here to be safe—I'm afraid to commit myself there—and the cab driver told me you could be trusted. I assure you I have no other motive than . . ." He smiled. There was something insane about him. ". . . than satisfaction."

She looked at the hundred and drew in a deep breath. When she hesitated, he took out his wallet and dropped another twenty on the stack. She nodded slowly. "Okay . . . how do I know when you want me to stop?"

He smiled and she noticed his eyes were green, kind of crazy green. "The way," he said, "you usually know."

She took the money and walked across the room to put it into her pocketbook. Turning, she slipped out of the robe.

He looked at her for a long moment. "Beautiful," he said. Then quickly, as though he had waited a long while for this, he jerked his tie free and tossed it over a chair. She had taken the rope out of the sack and put the towels along the end of the bed. "If I bleed too much, dab it with the towel. Just remember not to wound my neck, face, or lower arms."

She nodded, seeing that he was getting excited. He went to the bed hurriedly and rolled over on his belly and held his hands together behind him, ready for her. She didn't know a goddam about knots but she wrapped the cord tight until he indicated that it was good and she tied it the best she could. She tied his ankles to his satisfaction and wrapped the tape around them. Then she put three strips across his mouth and he nodded. Her hands were trembling as she took the needles and the razor blade. She could see the other scars where they had stabbed and cut him before. There were few places where there was not a scar, and she wondered how often he had done this. He lay perfectly still, waiting.

She clenched her teeth, took the razor, found a pattern established by some other prostitute some other time, and followed the same line. His body immediately stiffened and moans came from the adhesive tape as he began to agitate. Blood crept to the surface and oozed along his back as he writhed. The sounds he was making seemed to indicate he was urging her on to quicker, greater violence. The feel of the blade slicing into his body was bad. Very quickly she slashed him half a dozen times and he went into minor spasms, suddenly rolling over to expose his chest, which she also slashed several times, and she could see that this was it, that in spite of the hideous expression on his face, he was excited. He flipped over again and she took the pin in her fist and began to stab him, feeling like the vomit was going to burst from her throat at any moment, feeling the dizziness, the sickness as the moans came from under the tape.

He jerked his body fast, urging her on. In one hand she took the blade and in the other a pin and she worked on his back with both for maybe twenty seconds until she could see nothing but blood, and then his body stiffened, his neck thrown back, the muscles stretched like tight wires, and his eyes bulged as though in terror and, as she watched, it happened with a shudder, the eyes slowly, slowly closing, the face growing soft and gentlemanly again, and he went limp all over. She did not realize what she had done until then, until she tasted the blood and thought it was *his* blood somehow in her mouth, but she felt the pain in her lip where her teeth had closed on the flesh.

She dropped the blade and the pin and went to the wall and leaned against it, her face against the cool plaster for a moment while he lay soundlessly behind her. When she was able, she turned around and took the towels and began to dab at the blood on his back. She blotted for several minutes until the flow began to slow. He made a sound and she bent closer to his face and understood. She removed the binding from his hands and legs. He was still breathing deeply but gradually he caught his breath.

"There is some alcohol in the bag. Wet the towel and clean the wounds with it," he said, sitting up slowly, taking a towel to mop at his chest.

It took half an hour to completely stop the bleeding. The man dressed slowly, as though in a state of exhaustion. He tied the knot of his tie carefully, looking into the mirror, and slipped into his suit coat. Then he came across the room, around the bed where she stood still naked and sickened.

"Thank you, my dear," he said. He gripped her shoulders and kissed the side of her neck. As he drew away he smiled, at peace, ready to step into a classroom to say something maybe brilliant.

When he reached the door, he paused to survey the scene and, nodding slightly, opened the door and closed it behind him.

She looked at the bed, the blood, and went to the bathroom and turned the water in the sink, brushing it across her face with her hands, feeling the shudder, living the nightmare of the blood rushing to fill the trail left by the blade. She began to tremble, now that he was gone, like she was going to come apart. With her face wet, she left the sink and grabbed her robe, making a dash for Toby's room. When she reached his door she started to push it open but it was moving in front of her and she nearly fell. She was sobbing as he caught her in his arms.

"Oh, Toby . . . oh, God!"

"I know . . . I saw," he said, leading her to the bed and making her lie down. He poured her some liquor, added water, and told her to drink it. She stared at the ceiling for a while as he sat beside her.

"It was terrible," she said.

"Yes."

She didn't speak for a time but was comforted by his nearness.

"Why, Toby?"

She heard him exhale slowly. "You never know what's in a man . . . what he can do, what he does . . . what he thinks sometimes, back in his mind where he won't let anybody know. You don't know what makes him what he is and I suppose you can never know. No matter how long you know a man, you never know it all, and some of it—maybe a lot of it—he doesn't know himself."

The liquor began to take hold and she relaxed. He got up and turned off the light and then the light from the alley made large shadows in the room. She didn't even have to ask him. Didn't have to say a word.

"Go to sleep," he said. "Forget about it and go to sleep."

He lay beside her but he did not touch her. The hours passed and he did not move. Then when she was almost asleep, he crept away but not for long because she was still in that middle place before sleep when she felt his weight again on the mattress.

When she awoke, he was gone. It hit her again, the awareness, and she closed her eyes against it. Soon she crawled from the bed, her eyes swollen with sleep, and slipped on the robe. When she reached the room she saw that he had taken the bedspread away during the night. There was only one spot on the sheet where the blood had gone through, but he hadn't noticed that. Later that evening when he finished his work, he bought a bottle of good liquor and told her to get dressed up fit to kill and took her out for prime rib.

That was the only time she had stayed all night with him, that time. Because tonight, after he let her roll over on her stomach, with that nice drowsy feeling afterward, he let her rest for a time and said, "It's too hot, Roxie," and she knew, as before, that he was telling her to leave.

He was over there with his head near the window, his teeth out now and in the fruit box, the bottle maybe under his pillow, asleep, while she lay alone, watching the shadows from passing headlights on the street below. Down the block somewhere she heard voices late in the night, like coming from far across water, clear in sound, yet the words dulled and out of shape so she couldn't tell what they were saying. She closed her eyes.

So it was that way with Toby. She'd known it for a long time. Maybe it was never going to change, no matter what she did. She could take him that way or no way at all. She turned her head to feel the comfort of the pillow against her cheek.

"Sweetpot," she told herself, "no way at all is nothin'. Plain nothin'."

7

It had been a week, a long, hard week. To Toby it seemed infinitely longer. That past Saturday there was a relief from the heat. With the morning came the clouds, drifting and sinking, it seemed, until a fine drizzle moistened the sidewalks and streets except beneath the huge water oaks where the asphalt remained dry. But the sun was blotted out and the slight breeze from the north cooled. By afternoon the drizzle had stopped and, as they came in from their jobs, the pleasant weather, the weekly pay check, the Saturday feeling grew in them. They stripped away the work clothes and bathed or showered, those who could, and the others sponged from a bowl and added some sweet-smelling stuff and found in those dark closets the finery, yes, the plumage, and put on the starched white shirts and knotted the ties carefully, slipped into trousers, humming a tune perhaps, thinking about the ten dollars set aside for the evening, thinking about the black girls whose eyes they had caught before. Oh, yeah, a man could get himself drunk tonight and get that gal out and sweet-talk some and get some nice hot liquor in her belly to pre-heat the whole thing and . . . look out, man. Look out.

And somewhere a black woman sat before her mirror getting all ready, smiling at the image before her, doing her eyes this way and that, flirting, visualizing his broad shoulders and that nice trim waist, that loose way he walked, the feel of his arm hanging easily on her waist, nice and light, but there that big hand rested. *Gonna have me some good times tonight, baby.* And the white teeth flashed in the mirror . . . yeah, he'd reach out when the time was right and he'd pull her over there and he'd be gentle but right firm and the hand would come alive, slow and easy at first, like he was winding a clock he'd owned for years, and when he got it to running good . . . so good . . .

And as long as her husband didn't find out, or his wife or his woman or her man or her father, well, all right.

The cars began to slide in, bumper to bumper, before sundown, down New Hope Street in front of the liquor store, and those studs climbed out of the car and sauntered into the place, a thumb stuck in a belt as eyes surveyed the stock. Coming out with a brown bag, which you locked in the trunk if you were smart because the police didn't ask you to open the trunk, and if you did it was all right; they didn't bother you. Just don't have no bottle with a broken seal sitting on the seat between you and that black gal or you got to go downtown and blow up a balloon and maybe you drunk and maybe not—who in hell ever knew what they did with a balloon full of air—but then you got to post bond or let that little honey go home alone, if you were lucky, or got some help from some stud who most generously would take her off your hands while you were given a room for the night, courtesy the City of Yorksboro. No, that bottle went in the trunk for sure.

Toby trudged up the stairs and strolled down the hall. Curtis was sitting in his room. He wore a pair of slacks and no shirt, the windows open, enjoying the breeze.

"You got something planned?" Toby asked.

The kid turned toward him, holding a book. A Saturday night like that and he was lying up on a bunk holding a book. No hope for that boy. "I thought I'd read."

"Yeah," Toby said down in his throat. "You want a drink?"

"No . . . no, thanks."

Toby opened the bottle, a little over half a pint left, and took a short one. He wasn't drunk; somehow it hadn't come and, now on his second pint, that almost half gone, he was loose but nothing good. He looked to the end of the hall and saw Levi's door open and heard the television.

Levi was sitting in the big chair with his shoes off, his feet poked up on the windowsill. He had a can of beer in his hand and was watching a program intently. He was so hooked on television he watched anything. It didn't matter.

Toby entered the room and Levi waved him to a chair but did not speak because some cowboy was standing at the end of a bar and everybody in the bar had got real quiet and some other guy finished his drink in one swallow and pushed away from the bar, holding both hands out from his hips, the fingers curled to fit the butts of his pistols, and Levi took a quick drink of his beer, his eyes bulging some and his round fat face tense, like maybe one of those bullets might ricochet off the barroom wall and come right through the T.V. screen and he'd have to duck like hell or catch one himself.

"I don't want no trouble," the cowboy said. Levi nodded and Toby figured this had to be the good guy.

"Shoot his ass off," Toby said softly.

Levi frowned.

Toby prophesied that the bad man at the other end of the bar, who also stood with his hands out like that, away from his hips like he had tried to fart and discovered to his dismay that this was not what had been waiting in his bowels at all, figured that the bad man was going to say that the girl was his and anybody who wanted her had to take him first.

The other cowboy said, "You ain't gonna use that creek for waterin' your cattle no more. I got the right to it and that's all."

"But my herd . . ."

Toby said, "Fuck your herd."

The cowboy said, "That don't concern me."

Toby pulled the bottle from his hip pocket and put it on a small table beside the chair. He looked at it pleasantly. "Hey, Levi, I bet that guy wantin' the use of the water shoots the ass off the guy who won't let him use it."

"Toby . . . for God's sake." Levi took a quick drink of the beer, his eyes never leaving the screen.

"I bet he falls over backwards. He'll get him in the chest. They never shoot them in the head."

"Sssssshhhh . . . Toby."

Suddenly the television set burped the sound of gunfire. Toby did not look at the screen. He studied the shape of the bottle and wondered if, before it was too late, he might ought to get another one. "Hey, Levi."

Levi did not reply.

Toby ran his fingers over the shoulder of the bottle. "Who got shot?"

"You know." Impatiently.

"Did the bad man fall backwards?"

Levi nodded, not looking away.

"In the chest?"

Levi nodded.

"Is he dying?"

Levi nodded, trying to hear the dialogue.

"I don't see why that jackass figured the guy owed him the right to slop up all the water. Hell, he had legal rights to the place. If he didn't want the man to use his water . . . hell, the other guy could drill a well and put a windmill on the thing and pump his own water, but no, he wants this guy to *give* it to him out of brotherhood . . . he didn't even try to negotiate. That's why they all get killed; they don't negotiate. I mean how much . . ." Levi was giving up. Somebody was standing beside a grave and Toby assumed they were burying the bad man who wouldn't let the other guy have the water. ". . . how much would the guy have charged him to let the cattle drink anyway? He didn't even offer to pay him a little something for the water. I mean, maybe give him a few cows for the water if he didn't have ready cash."

The commercial came on the heels of the burial. That Toby liked. That got his attention because here came this black man carrying a briefcase, all decked up in a nice suit and a hat, strolling across an airline terminal and some high-yellow doll starts running up to him and grinds her hips against his pelvis and he gets his arms around her and they really take off for parts unknown in a cab, and he pulls out the cigarettes and they light up and she damned near has an orgasm when she exhales that smoke and he sits there with a shit-eatin' grin on his face, like he knew all along if she just took a drag of that cigarette he *had* her, but good. Maybe they used pot when they filmed it. Now *that* would be something.

Levi was drinking his beer. He didn't smoke anything but cheap cigars anyway and he had trouble identifying with this young, slim cat carrying the briefcase.

"You know what he does?" Toby asked.

"Who?"

"That guy on the commercial."

Levi looked at him absently.

"He's a lawyer. He's a big corporation lawyer. Or maybe

an advertising executive. They're good. He might even be a brain surgeon. I've never seen so many successful white-collar niggers in my life. Levi . . . we're gettin' there. You know that? All you got to do is look at the T.V. commercials and you can see niggers running the country and they all the time have beautiful women . . ."

Levi reached into a sack on the floor and took another beer which he popped open.

"Levi, how many times you seen a commercial with a nigger in a cotton field, and he stops with sweat runnin' down his back and neck and face and reaches into a pair of faded overalls and takes out one of those cigarettes and fires up and takes a big drag? Then some big fat nigger doll glides over and puts her hoe down and he gives her one and she fires up and, sweaty as hell, he puts his arm around her and . . . they're so wide together he has to walk down the row stepping on every other plant . . . to the bushes where they disappear. You ever seen that?"

Levi took a drink of his beer and smiled but his eyes cut to the set to see what was coming on next.

"You ever seen a garbage man, big black spade, dump a big load of garbage in a truck and step back and raise a cold bottle of Pepsi-Cola?"

"I don't reckon so," Levi said.

"You know . . . I just don't believe I can remember that either. We must make an assumption on that basis," Toby said. He drew a deep, contented breath. Levi tried to ignore him, so he raised his voice. "We must assume that what we are seeing on that screen is not a reflection of reality . . . or, if it is, not the broad reality. Or, on the other hand, if that *is* reality, we must assume that niggers in cotton fields don't smoke or drink Pepsi-Colas. And I am slightly per-plexed because . . ."

Dialogue came from the tube and Levi was leaning forward to hear. Somebody was giving a secret agent some orders and when he got through listening to a tape-recorded message, he put it in a garbage can and it caught fire all by itself and Toby wondered what would happen if the spy forgot what was on the tape . . . like he stopped in for a beer and met this chick and they shacked up for the night because the spy business could wait, only when he woke up he'd forgotten what the hell was on the tape and . . . Toby took the bottle and laid it in his lap. "Levi . . ."

Levi was miserable. He didn't want to miss this, but he couldn't be short with Toby—which Toby knew. He decided to let Levi enjoy his programs but he had to leave with one last observation. He went to the door and paused.

"Hey, Levi, you remember that commercial about using some kind of washing soap that made the washer ten feet tall?"

"Ummmmmm."

"You remember that? The washer shot up ten feet tall."

"Yeah."

"You know what I always wanted? I wanted it so bad sometimes I just prayed it would happen. Ask me, Levi."

"What did you want?" Levi's eyes were on the screen.

Toby grinned. "Levi, I always wanted that washer to shoot up like that, ten feet tall, in a room with a nine-foot ceiling." He giggled mirthfully and left Levi staring at the screen.

Roxie was downstairs in the bar, he supposed. He hadn't seen her for a couple of hours. He went into his room and put the bottle in the fruit box, deciding that he didn't much want another pint. If he got in a tight, Levi would have a couple of beers. He pulled his shirt free of his beltless trousers and unbuttoned it. Then he lay on the bed and pulled the shirt open across his chest.

For a few moments he thought about Roxie down there in

her Saturday evening dress, sipping along on a beer and waiting for those cats to start warming up. It would be a long night for Roxie. It would be a tired girl who climbed those steps the final time tonight. She would sleep late and do no business on Sunday, not because of the day or what it meant but because there wouldn't be any action—except maybe at the bad houses where it never stopped.

He closed his eyes and breathed deeply the cool air that came occasionally, like waves, through the open window. He let his body melt into the mattress and his mind drift lazily.

He was awakened as Roxie dragged some drunk clown along the hallway and he figured that would be some headache for her, the drunk one. He hit each side of the wall in the hallway a couple of times before he reached her room and went in laughing to himself about something he would never remember in the morning.

It was dark outside. Toby propped himself up on his elbows and drew a deep breath of cool air. He swung his legs over the side of the bed and stood. In the darkness he felt for the bottle in the fruit box and popped the cap, turning it up and swallowing. He didn't try for all of it the first time but he got enough that it burned all the way along. The saliva gushed in his mouth and he swallowed it, feeling a sudden numbness in his throat. He turned the bottle up again, knowing by the feel, by having turned up countless bottles like this, that there was one good swallow left which he took and sent down to join the other. He drew another deep breath and flipped the bottle through the open window, turning his head, immediately sorry he had done that because he was afraid that in the next instant he was going to hear somebody cry out, some guy standing out there in the alley feeling up somebody else's woman only to be slammed across the skull by a bottle that seemed to come from heaven. But he did not hear that. He heard it hit on something metal and knew, of course, that somebody had parked a car in the alley and it had landed on the car. Well, that would do very little damage.

He went downstairs and strolled into the bar. The clock showed eleven and the place was swinging. You could hear the band a block away with those guitars, amplifiers socked wide open, and those black singers about to swallow the microphones they clutched, yelling into them . . . something . . . *baby, baby, be good to me. Yeah.*

He pushed through half a dozen bodies, heading to the bar, and felt a soft buttocks against his hip and would have turned to see what that was maybe, but somebody got an arm lock around his neck and squeezed him and he heard, "Toby, baby . . . how you?"

He was released, whirled around, and moved like a ship in troubled seas toward the bar. They had three bartenders working and everybody was standing with money out and yelling over the sound of the music. Toby slapped down two quarters and caught the bartender's eyes. He nodded and in a moment a can of beer was on the bar and the quarters disappeared under a retreating black hand. *Now you see it; now you don't.*

Nadine fell or was shoved against him. "Hey, Toby . . ." and something else which he couldn't hear because the singer screamed into the microphone a long, wild shriek and the sound of the dancers came up to join the scream, so there was no telling what she said. He reached down and patted her fanny and winked. She nodded and her mouth split and he blinked into the glare of her teeth.

The noise was killing him. He took his can of beer and moved to the doorway where people were still coming in. He turned the can up three, maybe four times and it was empty. There was a table nearby so he put it on the table and went outside where it was cooler and stood on the sidewalk as people passed, looking at the young ones walking by who had been told how wicked that place was and how Mama had said not to go in there, and they wouldn't for a year or so and then they'd have to beat them with a brick to keep them away, some of them.

Toby moved along, up the hill, and when he reached the railroad tracks a block away he saw the black policeman standing there twirling his club expertly. He nodded to Toby. "Hey, Toby."

"How's it going?"

"I wish I was home," he said, letting his eyes search the sky.

"Big night?"

The cop nodded, his head toward the sound of the music which seemed like it would never run out. "I can tell by the sound that before it's over . . . long night."

Toby touched his elbow and plodded on up the street. He turned past the pawn shops, meeting a few people but not many now, and looked into the windows, seeing his reflection dimly, drawing in the sweet air. When he reached Cashua Street he slowed his pace and absorbed what was there, as he had done so many times, cruising around the courthouse square with his hands stuffed into his pockets, humming a tune for a time, then whistling softly, making the note quiver like he had done years ago when walking along with a girl, whistling softly . . . long ago.

When he had made the square, he was not finished. There was a kind of restlessness, so he took Cherry Hill Street and whistled his way for . . . he didn't count the blocks but he wasn't tired yet because of that long evening nap. He came to the hospital, the parking lot all but empty now, after visiting hours, but many of the lights in the rooms were still burning. He walked on, was crossing the street when he heard the siren coming from behind him. He paused and saw the red light flashing, the siren screaming hysterically. As the ambulance turned into the entrance, he saw an attendant hovering over the stretcher. He turned and followed along to the emergency door and when he arrived they had the door to the ambulance swung open and were lifting the stretcher out. The black man lying on the stretcher was saying, "Oh, Jesus . . . oh, Jesus," and his hand seemed to grasp his throat, until they took his hand away and Toby saw where the knife had entered from behind the neck and crept along, going deeper until somebody hit pay dirt, because the blood was flowing, forming a river down his neck to the white sheet. The attendant got behind the stretcher and gave those wheels a quick shove and swept the man into the hospital. Toby followed, seeing again the terror in the man's eyes as he tried to hold the blood inside his body with his hands.

Toby followed along the hallway and suddenly everybody, the nurses and orderlies, the hospital people were scurrying every way and a young nurse was asking the surgeon on duty to come as soon as possible, that the man was very critically injured.

They had wheeled the man into a cubicle and Toby could see through the glass as an orderly grabbed a towel and pressed against the wound. He watched the line of blood seep into the towel, more and more, and saw the man's arms coming up and down from the elbows and heard the man crying, "Jesus," and they were telling him to lie still, not to talk . . . that he was going to be . . . all right.

Toby imagined this guy and some other cat at the bar, facing each other as the others got back away from them, like on the television show, and maybe he said, "If she don't want to go with you, then man, cool it, hear? She's by God my woman. I'm telling you, nigger . . ."

And somebody went for the knife, probably both of them,

and the blade snapped open, a glimmer in the blue light from the bar, hard cold steel and—like a cat—that movement so swift it was hardly noticed . . . and it was over. He went down as the blood spilled out on that new suit and fancy knotted tie, and there were screams, like somebody had lighted the fuse on a bomb, because they all went different directions so that in less than a minute, even before the ambulance got started, there was nobody in there . . . just gone, like that, getting the hell out of there, except for the people who ran the place and they stood watching the circle of blood stain the floor.

He felt the hand on his shoulder. It was an orderly, one of the boys he'd seen around New Hope Street. He didn't know his name.

"Hey, Toby . . ."

Toby nodded. They had a bottle of blood hanging on a metal stand. A nurse got the man's arm stiff and was injecting the needle. In a moment she paused and looked to see if it was running into him. The doctor brushed by Toby, moving quickly into the cubicle. He tossed his coat to an orderly and rolled his sleeves two turns and stood over the man, examining. A nurse slid a tray beside him and he flipped open a wrapping and suddenly had on a pair of gloves, and then he grabbed an instrument and started doing something Toby couldn't see.

"Come on down, Toby . . . you want some coffee?"

"Yeah."

He got into the elevator with the orderly and it went down slowly and Toby did not speak. The door opened and they walked across the hall. A sign indicated that this was the morgue. He got a strange feeling as he entered. He hadn't known this was where the man worked.

He expected to see a body lying on one of the tables. Nothing. Clean white sheets. The man poured some coffee and handed him a cup, gesturing to a table. Toby remembered him then. He'd seen him once with Roxie. He had come in one night and paid her, but only once that he knew of. He wore a ring and probably his woman kept a close eye on him.

"May be a bad night," the man said.

Toby sipped the coffee.

"Had a car wreck a while ago. Man, his wife dead. They gone. They was dead when they got here. Run into a Trailways bus. Man, you want to run into something, don't pick no Trailways bus."

Toby really wanted to get out. He chatted a few minutes and was ready to put the cup down, half-finished, when the doors were shoved open behind him. He did not turn. Out of the corner of his eye he saw the stretcher appear, saw the sheet pointed sharply by a pair of oxfords. His host put down his cup and got up. In a moment the cart was removed from the room and they were alone.

The orderly pulled back the sheet. Slowly Toby raised his eyes to the table. There it was . . . again . . . so many pounds of matter, nothing else. Everything else was gone. His hand was not steady as he put the cup down on the table. The orderly paid no attention. He undressed the body in a very businesslike fashion. There were things he had to do, jobs he had to perform before the pounds of matter were released to a funeral home. The eyes and mouth were open. The terrible wound no longer bled but lay pink and exposed. An hour before, perhaps less, that . . . whatever it was now was laughing and stomping his feet and swaying wildly, alive, calculating his next drink or getting that woman out into the car with him to go someplace . . .

"He sure got cut," the orderly said.

Toby nodded but the man was busy and did not notice.

Why hadn't they negotiated . . . if it was a saucy black

woman . . . or the price of a beer . . . a borrowed lawn-
mower? The black woman could handle them all . . . there
was the price of another beer . . . what mattered so much
that a man stood like that with his hands at his sides, ready
to draw . . . a gun or a knife or what?

The doors swung open again and the police photographer
came in like he was very busy and this was intruding on
whatever it was he had to do. He photographed the body,
flashing the light into the dead face, close up on the wound,
and all the time the matter lay on the table and the open
eyes did not blink into the light. He was finished very
quickly. "Okay, he's yours," he said and went out the door.

"I'll be going," Toby said softly.

The orderly glanced over to the table where the steam still
crept from the coffee cup. "You didn't finish your coffee,"
he said.

"No . . . thanks." He went to the door.

"See you, Toby," the man said.

Toby nodded and took the stairs slowly, feeling his heart
labor in his chest. And he remembered what the doctor had
said and it filled him with dread, that perhaps with a faulty
heart and a bad liver, someday soon the orderly would be
standing over him doing those little jobs they do before they
turn you over to the funeral home, looking down into *his*
eyes, and what would be left would be nothing, nothing at
all but so many pounds of matter, and he felt sickened.
When he reached the top of the stairs he paused to get his
breath, sober now, and saw the woman in the red dress sitting there talking to the police officers and dabbing at her
face with a handkerchief, telling them what it was all about,
maybe. She was kind of fat and bulky from too many kids
and too many starchy foods, cornbread and beans and side
meat, and this was probably the only nice dress she owned
. . . and he had taken her out when he got his check cashed

. . . ten dollars for Saturday night. When she raised her arm to mop the tears, he saw that the breasts were large, straining against the brassiere outlined beneath the dress. When she unsnapped the brassiere they would fall. Her hair was messed now . . . she wasn't at all pretty, not before and certainly not now. And her man, or what had once been her man, lay within sixty feet of where she sat, his eyes staring out at whatever vision was his before that last, incredible moment. Between her sobs the officer, who was trying to be patient, who seemed to understand Negro grief, said softly, "Do you know the man's name? You said you'd seen him . . . can you tell us his name?"

At that she bent over and buried her face in her hands and the two policemen looked at each other. Toby couldn't hear what one of them said. He turned around and went out of the hospital, tracing his steps slowly back toward the glow in the sky that was the lights of downtown Yorksboro on a cool, pleasant, summer Saturday night.

And he hoped to God Levi had a couple of beers left.

8

On Sunday morning the sweat came long before dawn, nothing from the temperature because it was cool at the window, just a clammy sweat all over his body and he could feel his heart thudding in his chest. There were those two dead eyes staring at him when he allowed himself to think about it, thoughts which made bad feelings in his stomach. He could see the light coming to the sky and the clouds had cleared. It would be hot again by afternoon. There was practically no sound . . . an engine laboring away from the red light two blocks away on Cashua, groaning through a couple of gears, and then silence returned. Toby wiped the sweat from his forehead and as he sat up the muscles in his stomach vibrated like the strings of a harp, shaking his entire body. His breath was short as he walked to the orange crate and leaned his hands around it, against the wall where he let his head hang, closing his eyes for a time.

It was still too dark in the room to see. He felt along the bottom of the box and located the sack, tore it open, and removed the bottle of pills, the ones to relax him. He carried them in the palm of his hand across the room to the chair where he located his trousers, searching in the pockets for his lighter. He felt the shortness of breath . . . knowing that when it came it was like somebody holding your mouth closed and squeezing your nose so you couldn't breathe, knowing that a struggle took place inside and there was pain with it, a terrible gripping pain. So he drew in a deep breath to give his laboring heart some oxygen . . . *why was it when a man had a bellyful of liquor he didn't feel any of that?* If a man could feel that way all the time, he'd be all right, but come the morning . . . the headache was nothing . . . he used to think it was, but that was long ago. It was being on the verge of some internal disaster . . . the hideous anxiety . . . that was the thing, the internal terror that crawled like a snake through his chest. He remembered a crazy woman— anyway everyone said she was crazy, because she'd sit for a while and then start pushing down on her stomach, like to hold it down, and he found out that she thought there were snakes inside of her trying to crawl up around her neck, if they could sneak up that far, so she had to keep them pushed down. One of the boys on the block said she had this hang-up about sex, which was where the idea of the snakes came from. He didn't know. He never saw her anymore . . . maybe she was dead.

He found his cigarette lighter in the pocket of his trousers and let them fall back over the chair. As he flicked the lighter, he read the label on the bottle of pills by the flickering light from the flame. One capsule every three hours to relax. He snapped open the lid and let two of them roll out into his hand. At the sink he turned on the water and waited until the brown rust color had passed and the water ran clear, or so he assumed in the near-darkness. He put the capsules in his mouth and leaned forward, cupping his hand, like at a mountain spring, and swallowed until he felt the pills move down his throat on a journey to his stomach, where the gelatin would melt in the heat and the acid, then through the intestine, where the chemical would be absorbed, he hoped soon, so that whatever the pills could do they would do.

He went back to the bed and lay down, lighting a cigarette, which made the shaking worse in his hands and wrists and elbows. It was going to be a bad day. He turned his face and felt the stubble, the whiskers whistling across the sheet. The parade of faces came when he closed his eyes . . . so many already he had known, had drinks with . . . just gone now, not like they were dead, though he knew this, but like something had simply made them disappear. Sometimes he'd go into a place . . . once a small bar where they sold beer and sandwiches and there was a peg-legged old man behind the bar. He was there for years, like he'd always be there, but one day he came in and a new man was behind the bar, and when he asked he was told that Peg had died a couple of weeks before. But every time he went back in there he always expected to see Peg with his silver-capped tooth, grinning, "Hi, Mist' Toby." But no. He started wondering if Sal was dead. She'd be forty-one, wherever she was. Maybe she was dead. He turned his head to the side to get away from the thought, but the thought persisted. He tossed the cigarette out the window. He wouldn't want her dead and him not know it. But then he'd never accepted that she should be gone at all. He wasn't drinking that much in those days . . . just a pint, and he could hold that and go like fury the next day when he had to. That's what youth did for him. And if he had a headache, a Bromo fixed it right up, or maybe a beer about ten in the morning. And he didn't run around on her . . . maybe once or twice, but it was nothing, never anything serious. What kind of stud would it take to get her to run away like that? He'd imagined Harry Belafonte people all the time Danny was growing up. He hoped it was, because with a pretty man like that he could understand, but something told him it wasn't a man like that at all; it was probably just some simple spade who managed to turn her on like he hadn't been able to, and for whatever reason he'd never know because he'd had his share of praise from the women and not very much complaint. God, she was pretty, small and dainty-like and quiet. That was the part of her he never knew. That was what had been going on in her head the last few weeks, when she grew quiet, like she had her mind someplace else, which of course she did, and he'd have to repeat sometimes twice before she got back to reality, and he could remember laughing at how preoccupied she was, and she'd smile . . . and when he thought about it later he felt like a dumb ass . . . but what was there to be suspicious of? He didn't check on her. He didn't have any reason to, that he knew. No . . . she wasn't dead. Somehow he knew that. But he damned near was. He didn't have many of those sprees left in him. He was dried out, burned out in his chest and when he got to the top of the stairs he could feel it, just tired and burned out inside at forty-three.

Come on, pills, Let's have a little buzz here. Cool things down in there.

She wouldn't know when he died. If she was in Philadelphia or New Jersey someplace with that man, she'd never know. He must have been some man, whoever he was, to make her put the boy in the neighbor's house and leave. And never inquire at all. *Never.*

The light had come to the sky. A few noises could be heard outside, down the block, quiet morning noises like the slam of a screen door when somebody went out to get the Sunday paper . . . down the alley when a metal sound drifted along, like the lid of a coffee pot falling to the floor. *Well, you got to start someday.*

Toby crawled out of the bed and reached into the fruit box and took the book. He carried it to the bed and lay down heavily, letting out a low groan. He flipped open to the first pages, holding the book toward the window to catch the morning light. His mind was fuzzy from the liquor or the pills, maybe a little of both, and sometimes he had to read the same paragraph twice. His mind kept slipping away to other things. He'd always been a good reader. They had taken him from the second-grade up to the fourth-grade class when he was in school and they handed him the fourth-grade reader. He was supposed to shame the kids in the fourth grade who stumbled over the words, and he read it like it was nothing. He felt pretty big doing that, until on the playground one of the fourth graders called him a smart-ass shit . . . and then, college had been easy. He'd get a couple of quarts of beer and carry them to the room and lie there and study until it got late, getting a little drunk on a quart of beer in those days, but the next morning it would be there, what he'd studied. Toby smiled. If he'd wanted to do anything but paint, he might be one of those sweet cats with a briefcase . . . maybe Sal would have gone for that.

The print on the book came suddenly into focus when he thought of her. He disciplined himself and read until he could feel the print sneaking away from him and knew then that the pills were working. When he drew a deep breath, it came easier. He looked at the page number, committed it to memory, and slid the book under the bed, letting all of him go with the pills until the thought came that maybe with all that liquor in him the double dosage might kill him. He considered getting up and walking around, but he decided to take a gamble because the wave that came over his body felt so good. If he had to die, this was better than any way he knew, and if he didn't the world would wait for him right where it was. Nothing would change. Whatever that doctor had given him, he meant business, sure as hell. Vaguely he heard the kid speak from the doorway, probably on his way to get the morning paper to read about what was happening in the civil rights movement, grating his teeth over the Bill Buckleys and Kilpatricks columns . . . approving Carl Rowan and Sandy Reston . . . my God, there was more truth in the comic section than the whole lot thrown together.

He tried to answer. The kid said he was sorry, to go back to sleep, and he thought he must have got his arm up to wave a bit, and then after what seemed like a long while he realized that the kid had moved on. Maybe he needed to talk, needed to agonize over his part in the revolution, which it *was* to him. Toby was sorry. He'd get to it later. The revolution wasn't going to stop this morning. The kid's grandson would probably be worrying about it long after Curtis was dead. Dead.

That was the last thing he remembered until they were standing over him, the three of them. At first they were just forms, shapeless almost, ghostly, and he blinked, bringing them into better focus, drawing a long breath, feeling nothing hang up inside. He closed his eyes for a few moments, long enough for them to think he was going to drop off again, because Roxie said, "Toby . . . Toby."

He opened his eyes and the forms had really shaped up. They all looked concerned. He said good morning but nothing came out but a sound like a file sliding across some rusty metal. He cleared his throat and said it again. They looked at each other, Roxie in the middle, the kid on the left, and Levi on the right.

"Are you all right?"

He let a smile come to his lips. "Well, sweetpot, I've seen better days, I suppose."

"You were groaning and carrying on . . ."

"What time is it?"

"After twelve," Curtis said. He would know that. On a Sunday morning when it didn't matter what time it ever was, he would know.

"Light me a cigarette, Roxie," Toby said.

He stretched and felt the tremor in his muscles, but not like it had been before. He tried to remember when he had eaten last . . . a day, maybe two days. His stomach felt dry and shriveled. He wondered if he could get some food down.

Roxie took his fingers and placed the cigarette between them, but she'd been facing him and didn't know he was going to turn his wrist the other way when he took a drag, and suddenly he was wide awake, feeling the searing heat on his lips.

"Goddammit," he said softly. He sat up and Roxanne was comforting him, but he shrugged her away.

"You were talking," Levi said.

He nodded and tried the cigarette. It made him cough. He coughed for a long time until he almost vomited, but he swallowed that back.

"Who is Sal?" Roxie asked.

He raised his head until he was meeting her eyes squarely and he could see she wanted to know and she meant business.

"My wife," he said softly.

"Oh." Her face changed at that. She'd heard the story that his wife had left him, but it had been so long ago and maybe it didn't matter. She'd never heard the name and had never asked him before. She seemed relieved. Toby leaned back until his head was resting against the windowsill.

"You hungry, Toby?" Levi asked.

He nodded. "I'll go out in a while and get something."

"No . . . we was just goin'. You want us to bring you something?"

"Yeah." He gestured to his pants where the billfold was,

at least where he remembered it last. "A grilled cheese sandwich and a milk shake," he said.

They looked at each other. "I got some beer," Levi said.

Toby shook his head. "A milk shake. That's what I need." Levi had his billfold and was withdrawing a dollar bill. "Levi." Levi turned. "Tell the guy to put a raw egg in it. Stir it up good."

Roxie made a face.

As they started to leave, Toby remembered. "Curtis," he said, "did you want to see me?"

The kid waved it away. "It's nothing . . . I can talk to you later."

He listened to them going down the stairs and touched the burned place on his lip. If he could really feel anything, he figured that might be painful.

They were not gone very long. Levi presented him with the food and added that the apple turnovers looked so good he got one . . . had one himself, as a matter of fact. They stood watching him as he opened the cap on the shake.

"An egg?" he asked.

Levi nodded. Yes, an egg.

Toby unfolded the tissue around the sandwich, was about to take a bite when he glanced up to see them observing him intently. He hesitated.

"Don't you think it's possible?" he asked the group.

"What?" Roxie asked.

"That I can, unaided, with my own power, eat a grilled cheese sandwich."

The kid started backing to the door. "I'll see you later, Toby. I've got some reading to do." He waved and was gone.

Levi shrugged his massive round shoulders and without saying anything went to the door. Roxie tapped her foot on the floor for a moment, then came toward him and sat on the bed beside him. "Eat it," she said.

He ate, chewing slowly, because he did not want to so
astound his stomach that he caused any sort of upheaval at
this stage. He sipped the cold malt, feeling the balm slip
down his gullet to soothe the abused membranes. When he
finished he leaned back with his head against the windowsill
again. He could feel the food being received by his stomach,
could almost hear the response.

"Feel better?" she asked.

"Much." Which was not true.

"Are you out of liquor?"

"Yes."

"Levi said he could get you some while we was eating. If
you need it."

"Won't be necessary," he said casually, his voice almost
steady.

She lay across the bed with him and pulled her knees up,
making the skirt slide over her thighs. He looked at them
thoughtfully, silently studying the shape. From the alley he
heard a woman's voice raised in anger. She was giving her
man some hell for . . . probably Saturday night. They listened. She called him no good. He did not respond. She said
he was a goddamned sonbitch. There was no response for a
moment. Then he told her to shut up, but not very loudly
. . . they could just make it out. Toby shook his head. The
man had made a mistake. She cut loose. The language was so
classic he remembered it later. "You no-good goddamned
cocksuckin' son of a motherfuckin' shitass bitch."

Toby turned to Roxie and raised his eyebrows. "A mistake," he said softly, not wanting to miss what happened next.

"I tol' you to shut up."

"I'll kiss your stupid black . . ."

That's all she got. It sounded like he hit her with a chair.
It was silent then and Toby became genuinely alarmed until
he heard her begin to cry. He had taken it out of her. He

hadn't wanted to. He'd let it go as long as he could, but the time came. And the anger was out of her good because she didn't stop crying right away and go back into the rage as she sometimes did, so that he had to hit her again. The sound now came from another part of the apartment. When she continued to cry, Toby knew she was not finding a knife. She really was through for a while, at least for the weekend. He would sit there, maybe smoke two cigarettes, and then he'd go in and cuddle her some and she'd cry again and, probably, if he didn't do it all the night before, he'd make love to her.

"Was she pretty?" Roxie asked.

Toby turned to her. The face he saw was light, nicely angular, but the eyes very dark. He took a cigarette and offered her one. She waved it away. He lighted it and exhaled. It caused a bad feeling in his stomach.

"No . . . not really pretty. Nothing beautiful like you."

"Hell," she said, pleased.

"You've seen yourself. You know what you got," he said. "Don't knock it."

"I always figured she was special . . . maybe real pretty." He did not reply. She took a deep breath and from the corner of his eye he saw the breasts rise and fall. "Did you love her?"

"Yes."

She didn't like that too much perhaps, but as long as she came before, it didn't matter all that much. She waited a long while. He was not sure how far she was going to try to go with it. "Do you love me?"

He pushed away from the windowsill and went to the fruit box where he shook one of the red pills from the bottle. He turned on the faucet at the sink and popped the pill into his mouth, bending, swallowing the water that ran over his cupped hand. He tilted his head back and it went down.

"What was that?"

"A pill."

"Goddammit, I knew that. What for?"

Toby ran his hand across his chin. The whiskers were stiff. "To relax me."

"You were pretty relaxed last night."

"Yes." He sat down and listened to her voice coming from behind him.

"Are you sick, Toby?"

"I'm forty-three years old. I drink too much," he said.

"You been doin' that for years. Hell, you can go on forever."

He did not respond to that.

She did not pursue it further. In fact, he thought she had forgotten how it all began, but she was a smart little cookie. "Toby . . ." He felt her hand rest against his neck. "Do you love me, Toby?"

He smiled. "Roxie . . ." he said. "Do I ever ask you that?"

"You don't have to. I tell you." That was not true.

"You've had men tell you that before, haven't you? They said it . . . sometimes they said it real good, lots of sweet talk . . . jellied you up all inside."

"Yeah."

"So what happened?"

"One of them hit me in the mouth. Another one tried to burn my breast with a cigarette."

"Didn't mean much then, did it?"

"No . . . but a woman, if she's got a man . . ."

He leaned back and closed his eyes. Her hand was still against his spine, comfortable. "What you really want to know, Roxie, being a woman, is did I love her more than I love you. That has been working around in your head for a long time and especially the last hour and a half. And I say to you, dear, that the asking of the questions is a bad sign. It suggests a possessiveness that is disturbing to a man in my position."

"What are you saying?"

"When you are forty-three, you will understand about the other . . . and my son . . . you will understand about us. What we have now is obvious and lovely and if you don't shut up you will talk it to death."

This apparently was the reassurance she needed because she squeezed him with the hand at his back and snuggled against his shoulder and said very softly, "You no-good goddam cocksuckin' son of a motherfuckin' shitass bitch."

He could feel the pill taking up where the first two had left off. "Now turn around and we'll take a nap," he said.

She slid around next to the window and he lay beside her. "Really a nap or . . ."

"Really a nap," he said.

"Okay, baby."

He closed his eyes and she very gently laid her hand on top of his. That was the last thing he remembered. When he awoke she was gone.

He did not go downstairs the following morning to open the shop. He went down twice on Monday, briefly, to eat, returning to the bed where he read at length from the book, and when the three hours were up he took a red pill.

Roxie came up the stairs, panting, to tell him somebody was down there wanting some signs.

"Tell the man I'm sick. I'll be there later."

She frowned. "When later?"

"Just later," he said.

She must have discussed his behavior with Levi and Curtis because they, in turn, asked about his health.

"I'm taking a small vacation. Even a nigger sign painter deserves a few days rest."

Levi was pained by the word. He never liked to hear Toby say it. He tolerated it, but barely.

The kid poked his head in and asked if he had seen a doctor. Toby assured him that he had. But they kept walking up and down the hallway . . . he thought, more than need be, slowing to peer into the room, until it became too dark for them to see. Roxie came in guided by the glow of her cigarette.

"Levi wants to know if you want a beer. He'd come down, but he's watchin' something on the television."

Jesus God. If he wasn't drunk, they got uneasy. "No, I'm fine. I've taken twenty of those red pills and in a few minutes I'm going to sleep and never wake up."

The light came on overhead, the bare bulb blinding him. "For God's sake, turn that thing off."

She went to the fruit box and took the bottle of pills, seeing that more than half remained.

He closed his eyes. "Now turn off the light," he said.

"You need a shave."

"Yes . . . turn off the light."

"You didn't take a lot of pills."

"No."

"Why the hell you say a dumb thing like that?"

He chuckled. "Roxie . . ."

The light went out. "Are you going to sleep?"

He watched the glow of the cigarette in her hand, moving about, almost like a conductor directing a slow movement, very graceful. "Yes."

"That's all you've done. When you gonna get up and shave?"

"I haven't decided."

"I don't get this at *all*."

He turned his back to her and faced the window.

"You want me to stay awhile?"

"Yes, until you can tell I'm asleep."

She lay beside him.

For the first time, he was able to bring up the dead man. "I was out at the hospital Saturday night," he said. "They brought a man in . . . I've seen him around but I didn't know him. He got cut. I went downstairs and—it was the morgue—and I was drinking coffee and they brought him in dead. Was that at the Blue Heaven Bar?"

"No," she said. "I heard about it. It was across town. I think he was in one of them bad houses."

"Oh." For some reason, that relieved him. For an instant he saw the dead open eyes and he shook his head to get it away.

"Man's a fool to go to one of them places," Roxie said.

"Yeah."

"You don't go no more, do you?"

"No."

"They get all high on somethin' . . . they don't make no sense."

"That's right. Goodnight, Roxanne."

She nuzzled against him and kissed his ear. "God, you need a shave."

On Tuesday he got up at nine-thirty, took a pill, and stood before the mirror. The shakes, for the most part, were gone. He went to the sink and ran some water and sprayed lather into his palm. He drew the razor carefully across his face, then went down the hallway and climbed into the shower, letting the water run across his face and eyes, savoring the cool feel as it rushed over his body. His legs were somewhat trembly but much better than the day before. He dressed in clean clothes and went downstairs. After a small breakfast, he opened the door to the sign shop. Some mail had been shoved through the slot—nothing much. One sign order. A lawyer wanted his name on the door when Toby could get around to it. Fine.

He opened a jar of red sign paint, selected a brush, and dipped it into the paint, feeling the tremor, though not really as bad as he'd figured. He took an old sign and leaned it against the easel. Carefully he shaped the S. It wasn't, he decided, very good. He tried again. For half an hour he kept working. He could get by with it, but it wasn't as good as he liked. Another sign painter could tell it was shaky. He looked at the lawyer's name and saw that it had no S's in it. He determined that with one of the red pills, by mid-afternoon, a young lawyer would be in business.

The man had been standing in the doorway for a while. Toby turned. It seemed that the man had considerable poise, his hands folded in front of him, his head cocked to one side.

"Good morning," the man said. Toby nodded. He was old, maybe sixty-five, with gray hair and pale skin. "I noticed the painting. Is it yours?"

Toby followed the white man's gaze to the painting of the one-eyed doll in the garbage can. "Yes."

The man came into the shop and walked over to the easel which held the painting. He examined it carefully, adjusting his bifocals with one hand. "I was by here the other day . . . someone said you were on vacation."

"Yes." Toby ran his hand over his chin as the man continued to study the painting.

"Is it for sale?"

Toby took a cigarette from his shirt pocket, picked it clean from the pack, and lighted it.

"I'd like to buy it, if it is," the man said.

"I see," Toby said.

"What are you asking?"

"I haven't thought about it," Toby said. But he did then. He got to visualizing fifty dollars. He looked at the man's clothing. Nice suit. Shined shoes. "I haven't thought about it," he said again. "I don't do much painting anymore. That one . . ." he paused for a moment, "is something special to me."

The man turned slowly. Maybe he'd heard that before. He drew out his wallet—not from the hip pocket, from the coat pocket, a long, thin thing. "Then may I make you an offer?"

Toby bobbed his head.

"I offer you a hundred dollars."

Toby had brought the cigarette six inches from his mouth when he heard it, and he stopped there, his eyes narrowing. He looked into the man's face a long moment, then cut his eyes to the painting, to the face of the ruined doll, but more than that . . . he looked into the face until the man said he thought it was a fair offer. Toby turned away, flicking the ashes to the floor. "It's not that," he said.

The green came out of the wallet. "I'll give you a hundred and twenty-five dollars," the man said, ready to count it out on the table.

There were two or three other paintings in the shop. Toby got up and turned them around so that the man could see them. "Is there anything else I've done . . . ?"

The man looked at the other paintings quickly. "No . . . they're fine, understand, but this one . . ." he pointed with the money, "it has something. I especially want this one." He had made up his mind.

Toby went back to the stool. "No," he said. "I don't think so."

"I've gone as far as I can go," the man said. "As far as I think I should."

"I'm not playing with you," Toby said.

Their eyes met briefly. "No . . . I don't think you are." He pushed the money back into the wallet. From another section he withdrew a card. "I live in Charlotte. This is my card. If you change your mind, Mr. Snow, call me."

Toby took the card and placed it on the table beside the easel. He got up to follow the man to the door. "If you bought it," he asked, "what would you do with it?"

"Hang it in my home. And when I die, I'll give all my paintings to a museum in this region."

Toby nodded. "I see."

"Think about it," the man said.

"Yes."

Then he was gone. Toby turned and walked to the painting. He tried to imagine it among all those abstract things . . . a museum. He had the impulse to run out and catch the man, if it wasn't too late. But he didn't move. He sat on the stool. *How do you like that? For God's sake!*

In half an hour Roxie came in.

"Hey, sweetpot," he said.

Her face brightened. She pulled a chair up beside him and looked at the lettering, but she wouldn't know a good S from a Z.

He put the brush down and took the man's card from the table. "Listen, Roxie . . ." He waited until she looked into his face. "You see this card?"

"Yeah."

"If I were to get drunk and step in front of a milk truck or something . . ."

"Toby, for Christ's sweet . . ."

"Listen," he said patiently, "I want you to keep this card. And if something happened to me, I want you to call this number and ask for this man. He's an insurance man in Charlotte. He'll pay you a hundred and twenty-five dollars for the painting of the doll."

"He offered you that?"

"Yes."

"Toby . . . God-a-mighty, Toby." She threw her arms around him and gave him the treatment, then slowly relaxed. "Why the hell didn't you take it?"

"Well . . ." He shrugged. "It was close, but I figure I'll wait for a while. Just in case something . . ."

"Don't, Toby. I don't like to hear that talk."

"All right. But you keep the card. It's important to me because he said he would put it in a museum someday."

"Son of a bitch!" she said.

Toby got up and began to put the paint and brushes into his kit. When he had what he needed, he snapped it shut. "I'll be back. I've got a little job. If you aren't busy, I'll buy you a sandwich."

His legs weren't entirely steady, but he was all right. By God, he was all right. When he reached the door he paused.

"Don't lose that card now."

She came up beside him and pulled her blouse out with one hand and most provocatively slid the card down into the brassiere. Then she raised her eyes, the lids lazy, until she met his eyes.

He slapped her lightly on the fanny and went up the street toward the railroad tracks. And he did not notice that the grade made him breathe very hard.

9

At ten o'clock the traffic had thinned outside the shop as the darkness and the hour called home the weary for rest to face tomorrow. Toby sat in the shop at the desk with his feet up, leaning back in the chair and sipping an orange soda pop that had grown warm as he smoked. He closed his eyes wearily for a long moment.

He could feel the juke box from the bar down the street. When the bass notes sounded, they caused a small vibration and he was not sure whether he was feeling or hearing the sound. Odd how those screaming high notes got lost in space but the deep low notes kept moving. Many nights he had lain in the bed upstairs feeling the deep notes come through the building like a pulse, steady, rhythmic.

He thought perhaps he might do another painting, steady now after almost two weeks of sobriety. Somehow all the ideas he'd had when he was drinking those years before had vanished. The soul things, the things that told the story of his people, all of those images . . . what was it? . . . a vision he'd had of an old Negro woman laboriously climbing the steps of the AME church, stabbing with a cane and holding with a thin and withered hand to the iron railing that, foot by foot, led her to the sanctuary and worship. Eighty years old and weighing perhaps eighty pounds, but filled with a fierce determination to reach her destination, and in her tired old eyes a kind of faith that was awesome. Saved, she was, and she knew it. Her God. Even as drunk as he was that morning coming back from a house where he had spent the night, Toby had paused to study her face. If he could only remember how it was. It was gone, somehow, out of focus now.

He had visualized Roxie, her face close like she was after he'd made love to her, all the desire gone, satisfied and sometimes satiated, her drowsy eyes quietly intent on his face, saying more with that expression than if she'd talked for hours. It occurred to him that perhaps this was her faith, the magic of the church that is a part of the body, the male.

And his? His God was dead. Temporarily at least, and he told himself, perhaps with reservation, permanently. Four ounce-and-a-half shots of hard liquor, that was where old God had hidden for so long. He remembered a black prostitute from years before, past her prime by several years, not getting many tricks and suffering something terrible trying to support her habit, which was morphine. When she could get it, shot all to hell, lying on a couch in her room, about half gone on the last injection, and she said, "Toby, everybody's got to have something. You know . . . you can't cut the scene if you don't have something, the sauce or pills or a man or . . . something. It's too much, Toby . . . just too goddam much."

And that was what Bill said when he dropped by to see about Toby. "You doing all right?" he asked, pulling up his trousers so that when he sat down the creases would not be spoiled.

"Better," he said.

"You looked like you'd have a few hard days."

Toby nodded. "I had some pills. They made it easier."

Bill talked about taking it easy and living one day at a time and being grateful that he got through the day without bombing out. After a while he fired up a cigarette and told him something that he was always experiencing. "It's like," he said, "you lost a contact. That liquor had been the thing, the way of life so long that when you cut it off, you feel stranded. Like you don't know what to do with yourself. You've got to replace all that with something . . . partly this program, working this thing out, and partly with work . . . so you don't get to thinking about the good times, the times before the liquor got to hurting so much."

That made good sense, Toby thought. He stayed away from the bar down the street because the smell of the beer nearly drove him crazy, and he must have eaten a hundred candy bars when he felt shaky, his body craving the sugar. And he worked. He even went out on the street and solicited business and got some. One day he impulsively bought Roxie an armful of expensive underwear, a French bra . . . she liked that, with her cleavage . . . all that bikini stuff they were wearing. And she acted like a kid on her tenth birthday. But still time dragged, seemed to mope along. When it grew dark and he was alone up there, he became restless and couldn't decide whether to take a walk or go downstairs and try to paint something with soul, maybe worth a hundred and twenty-five to that man in Charlotte. He felt a little proud of himself, though there was no one to talk to, not about that, except Bill and he'd seen him only a few times. He hadn't called him. As long as he was all right . . . the man had a family. No use to bother him. And he could imagine how a white man felt somewhat uncomfortable down here.

"You busy, Toby?"

He turned in the chair, keeping his feet on the desk. Ol'
Julius Bigger stood in the doorway, a long, thin man with a
head that looked like his mama had sat on it, flattening the
thing so his eyes seemed sometimes too close. His face was
serious now as he stood looking into the shop, the muscles of
his body drawn and his fists balled up. Toby could feel the
tension.

"Come in, Julius," he said.

The lawyer slapped his heels on the concrete floor as he
came across the room, pulling at a chair and sitting abruptly,
letting out a quick short sigh, his teeth locked together.

"I don't have a drink for you tonight," Toby said. "Except
some orange soda pop. You want some?"

"No," abruptly, then with thought, "thank you anyway."

Toby drew the bottle to his mouth and took a swallow of
the sweet liquid. "What's the matter, Julius?"

The lawyer crossed his legs and Toby looked at the near
bones underneath. "Toby, I've reached a decision."

Toby waited, toying with the orange soda and looking at
the bare canvas he'd leaned on the easel, thinking briefly of
the face of the old woman climbing the church steps. He
wished he could think of something else like some of them did,
like his mother had done when his father would get on one
of those righteous tirades, all hung up on God. She'd just go
on ironing and make a sound in her throat, when he paused,
to make him think she was taking it all in, and that satisfied
him. She'd heard it God knew how many times before and he
never seemed to do anything but repeat, sometimes in different words, the same old hang-up . . . which was what ol'
Julius was going to do, sure as anything, just go back over
the same old frustrations with the same old incredible re-
sponses. So Toby made the small sound in his throat to tell
Julius to go on.

"There isn't any way. They've either got to give us a nation of our own or we can't go on."

Toby tasted the orange soda. It was sticky to his lips. *Why* couldn't they go on? He did not ask.

"But, Toby," Julius leaned forward conspiratorially, "they won't give it up easy."

"Give what up?" he asked, thinking he had asked the same question a couple of weeks or months ago, the last time this agony was discussed.

"The land . . . the territory."

"Oh."

"So I've reached a decision. Toby . . ." He pointed a long, trembling finger. There seemed to be no meat on the finger, the flesh stuck to the bone like a layer of black paint. "We've got to get guns." Julius kept the finger aimed at his heart for a long moment. Then he bobbed his flattened head and repeated. "We've got to get guns."

Toby looked away, peered at his shoes, dusty, all wrinkled from wear, molded to fit his feet comfortably. Then he thought that he had seen that golf player on television, bent over a putt, one Sunday afternoon in Levi's room, trying to sink a six-foot putt, and the camera had zeroed in on the ball and he saw the man's foot, could see him wiggling his toes inside the shoes to relieve the tension. He wiggled his own toes and watched the leather move and pursed his lips, listening to a car cruise by outside, then drew a deep breath, wondering what time it was and how long Julius was going on with this, wondering what Roxie was doing, hoping maybe she'd come in and interrupt, get sassy and tell ol' Julius that what he needed was a good piece of ass to forget that trouble for a while . . . and exhaled the breath of air as Julius let that gun business sink in.

"What would you do, Julius?" He listened to his voice and realized that Julius, the kid, Roxie, sometimes even Levi and

God knows who else up and down the block used him, that
if he were a psychiatrist and these people had any money,
he'd be making a good living. They came back because he
didn't fight with them, didn't get mad, just sat there and took
it all in, let them vent it on him while—until recently—he
sipped on his liquor and was loose and easy. That was why
they came back. He didn't ever really agree with them, or at
least not often, never argued heatedly while he sipped the
liquor . . . you live and let live, you do your thing, whatever
it is, and you get what there is to get . . . you fight the narrowing road as long as you can . . . you live, you meet each
day hoping for God's sake that something, some experience
will come out of it that is good. And he thought that most
of the good had been the feeling in his head when he got
those four or five ounces of liquor down there. Hell, *he* had
a reason to be mad. He had a wife who left him and a dead
son. He'd had the experiences of the street, the indignities
. . . the cop throwing his ass in jail, sometimes when he
wasn't even drunk, just out doing his walking and maybe
drifted into a white neighborhood, and they drove up and
asked what that nigger was looking for over there in the
white part of town . . . and the charge always stuck. He'd
learned that. You sleep in the jail and go up before the city
judge and plead guilty and don't argue with the white cop
because that judge would back that cop up every time, and
the more you argued the bigger the fine or the longer the
sentence. But Sal and the boy . . . the box and the flag and
the soldiers firing over his body . . . the trouble . . . none of it
had made him bitter. When nobody wanted his paintings, as
he gave up slowly, he accepted that it didn't really matter all
that much, that life was a series of sensations and most of
them that mattered were physical or could be manifested by
some physical reaction . . . that he could be famous even and
it wouldn't matter, if the sensations were bad. You didn't

have to be a big man to savor the sensations, when that first good belt of liquor crept down there to start the magic, a woman's hand on his belly, like a snake dozing but ready to move . . .

"What," he asked softly, "would you do with guns?"

"We'd make Whitey listen. Organized, like we're planning, they wouldn't know what hit them. Nothing stupid. Toby, we'd go out and blow up the power stations . . . like teams of commandos. We could paralyze this country and keep it immobilized . . . communication, transportation, all of it, for as long as it took, until the white man looked around and decided he'd get out cheaper to give us our nation."

"I see," Toby said. "They were going to blow up the Statue of Liberty sometime back."

"A symbol," Julius said, "that was all. We wanted to show them we could do it and destroy that phony symbol."

Toby took a drink of the orange and put the bottle on the table. "They got caught," he said carefully. "Seems I remember they got caught before they got it done."

"Yes."

"How do you suppose they got caught before it happened?"

Julius said nothing.

"Julius, you don't suppose they've got government men inside all those outfits, in every gang, every Panther group . . . and when something gets started, like they're going out to blow up Niagara Falls or something, this guy makes a phone call and the commandos get there and, before they can even get ready . . . it's all over."

Julius didn't like that. Briefly he seemed disturbed that a black man might betray his own people to the establishment. "That may be, but it's changing. You get a man at the top, he sends out six groups, you see. If there was an informer, he'd know what the group he was in was planning, but there would be no way for him to find out about the other groups. The man might be able to stop that one operation, but he couldn't stop all of them . . . one out of six or seven bombings, but it would be timed to happen all over the country at once. We could bring them to their knees. They aren't tough anymore. The white middle-class has gone soft. They are so comfortable they would make peace at our price to keep from losing what they have."

"You don't suppose the black man would be outgunned?" Toby asked. It wasn't as easy sober. The tension crossed the line, got into his mind. He moved his toes to send it out the other end of his body.

"They wouldn't know who to get. The commandos would strike and be gone. They'd go underground. All the white man could do is call out the Guard after it was over. And it would be quiet for a while and then they'd strike again, and all the time our people would be negotiating from strength . . . to build our nation. Listen, Toby, the boys back from the war, Whitey taught them all the tricks of the trade so they could fight the war for him . . . and he doesn't forget; he knows all about it. We've got ammunition, explosives . . . you wouldn't believe what we've got ready when the time comes."

Toby visualized the nation. Where was he going to buy the paint and brushes for his signs? What paper plant was going to produce the cardboard? He couldn't very well imagine the white man providing the technology for the black nation . . . but he was weary of it now and he determined to ask no more questions.

"I don't know," he said.

"You'll live to see it, Toby. It won't be long."

A sinking feeling drifted around the orange soda that was being absorbed by his stomach. Because struggle as he might, do whatever he had to do, there was a damaged heart inside his chest from hard wear, and a liver nearly gone and he had to face that ugly reality even as he fought it . . . that in the end it's a losing proposition, that you get old, slow or fast . . . it comes and a man disintegrates, goes down, and the only glory to it at all is that he goes down with some courage or dignity, that he drags his body up and makes it go on as long as it can, makes it perform, gets glasses and teeth and hearing aids and pills to expand the blood vessels or to make the kidneys function, because he *has* to hope. Pitiful. Running until he cannot run any longer, then walking, fast at first, then slower, and hobbling later, like the old woman with the cane, and then grasping to life, bedridden, hoping, struggling until the end. What put that in a man? His mama didn't teach him that. Where did it come from?

He took his feet from the table and turned in the chair. He rested his hand on Julius's bony knee and met his eyes squarely. "I don't know," he said gently. "You may be right."

"We're right," Julius assured, the face going softer now that he had spilled the venom, had fed it into Toby's mind. The long fingers lay relaxed in his lap. He must have been dreaming of cities without electricity, water supplies poisoned, and the white man defeated, ready to sign an armistice giving Julius Mississippi and Alabama and Georgia.

Toby patted the knee and leaned back. Upstairs the kid was poring over studies in sociology about how this community or that had managed to integrate . . . how if everybody pulled together they could make it. The white kids could get on a bus and ride to the black schools and they got along fine . . . how the people in one California residential district got the first black man in there, how they had meetings and agreed they would not panic or sell the houses, and how after three years nobody thought about it anymore and it hadn't turned all black like a tide of oil seeping down the street, the whites fleeing before it. Curtis the Kid could find some study to show how industry was soliciting black executives, hiring all they could get, running ads in *Ebony* . . . *We Want You* . . . *Join Us* . . . how even a black man could take a white girl to the theater, even in Maryland, and nobody said much anymore. Poor Curtis, going one way so hard and fast, while Julius went the other way just as fast. All worried and passionate, tied up inside about those things, and missing the sensations, the life experiences, an ol' catfish creeping away with a crawdad on the end of the line . . . a woman looking at him that way. He remembered when he was a kid, maybe ten, he and some of the others had been out that evening, playing around the streetlight; when they started home, they saw through the side window of a house an old man, seventy probably, though he could not remember now—he had seemed seventy, all wrinkled, the muscles in his arms gone out of shape, flabby, going to pieces and not much time left—hovering over the woman who was nearly as old and doing everything he could to get an erection . . . one more time, hungering to feel one more time the heat in his loins. He might have made it and he might not because they heard footsteps on the sidewalk and ran, but the old man was going for the life experience and nothing else mattered to him at that moment. If he made it that night, the next day he'd come out and sit on that porch in the sunshine and let the warmth seep into his bones and smile pleasantly, watching the young girls go by and thinking of that indescribable response in the brain that he had had once more.

Julius stood, the joints creaking almost audibly. "Best I go on. It's getting late."

Toby took the remaining inch and a half of orange soda and drank it, setting the bottle down on the table. He followed Julius to the door. The beer sign down the street indicated that it was ten-thirty. He turned the lights off and locked the door. They paused together on the sidewalk, listening to the sounds of the city growing sleepy.

Julius's face reflected the intermittent green and red neon light from the beer sign. "Goodnight, Toby," he said. "Come over to see me."

"Yes," he said.

He watched the figure recede down the sidewalk, moving over to let a pair of young lovers pass, his head down, full of plans for the day of the revolution.

Toby turned to the stairway and climbed slowly, breathing a bit heavily as he neared the top. He moved quietly into his room, deciding against the light. He removed his keys, the cigarettes and lighter and put them in the fruit box. He lay down on the bed with his hands folded behind his head and wondered if those young ones would commit themselves like Julius believed. How many of them would die at eighteen or twenty not knowing the things that his body had known, cheated, giving themselves for something they would not be around to enjoy, if there was anything left to enjoy? Then he turned it in the other direction, the young white woman sleeping beside her black man, and he wondered how long it would be before such a woman could send her little brown child to school and not have to face a kind of silent castigation.

Roxie came along the hallway in the dimness of the forty-watt bulb, leading a man, a big man, Toby thought . . . the way he walked made the boards sigh beneath his weight.

He got up and found the pills and shook one into his hand. He swallowed it at the sink and was unbuttoning his shirt when he heard the sound, an angry sound . . . deep, low-pitched . . . and because he could interpret the meaning of the sound, he cocked his head toward her room. There was another sound, an impact that might have been flesh on flesh. He moved to the wall between the room and opened the panel. Roxie was on her back trying to scream, but the man had one hand around her throat and he was bouncing up and down on the bed, getting a better grip with his big hand and beating her in the face with the other one. She clawed at him with her nails, unable to scream, fighting to breathe.

Toby felt in the darkness quickly, locating the baseball bat in the corner. He tried to turn the corner so fast that he hit the door frame and prayed to God she hadn't let him lock the door, which he had told her never to do, and slammed into the door with his body as he turned the knob.

"Stop it!" He heard a sound near panic that had come from him.

The black man turned abruptly, still choking her, and Toby rushed across the room, the bat cocked, ready to catch him on the back of the head, and saw the hand come away from her throat and heard her draw in a hideous breath. The man was huge, built like a fighter. Toby got between the man and his trousers, the bat still cocked for the swing. The man rolled off the bed and stood facing him, his arms coming up in front of him as if to grab the bat, and Toby took long breaths because he could feel the pounding in his chest, and said, "You make one move and I'll split your head."

The man's mouth was open, the lip hanging down as though he might drool. His chest was heaving, the eyes blind with rage, but he kept looking at that bat and he must have known Toby would break his head open if he moved at all. Roxanne had pulled up on her elbows, still gasping for air, and there was no time to waste.

"Roxie, come over here." Her hand was at her throat. She did not move. "I said get up and come over here behind me."

She got up, still holding her throat, and moved behind him.

"Get in those trousers," Toby said to the man. "If he's got a knife or . . ."

Roxie's voice failed her. She tried to make a sound but was

not able. Toby felt the solid metal against him. He took a step back and quickly took it from her hand. It was a pistol, a twenty-two, short barrel. He handed her the bat with his other hand while he leveled the pistol on the man.

"Get dressed," he told her.

She found the robe and he glanced at her very briefly and saw the eye and cheek swelling already. He moved away another step.

"Did he pay you?"

Still unable to speak, she nodded.

"Give me the money."

She frowned.

"Give me the goddamned money," he shouted.

She went to her purse and took out the bills, staying far away from the man. Toby took the bills from her and crumpled them in his hand. He threw them on the floor at the bare feet of the man. The man had loosened some, not as ready to leap, now that Toby had the gun.

Toby turned to Roxie as he eased across the room. "Get out of here. Tie that robe and get out. Go outside . . . someplace."

She left the room, able to breathe more easily now, touching the side of her face.

Toby felt the tension easing. He pointed with the pistol. "Pick up the money and put your clothes on," he said evenly.

The eyes on him were quiet now but deadly cold. The man did not alter his gaze for some time. Then he bent down and took his underwear as Toby eased toward the door. In a few minutes he was dressed. He collected the bills and stuffed them in his pocket.

While he was dressing, Toby remembered him. Sonny Hutto. They'd talked about him on the street. He was in the penitentiary for a murder his lawyer managed to get reduced to manslaughter. It was, they said, not the first man he'd killed, just the first they'd caught him for. People gave him a lot of distance. Toby didn't know what had made Sonny go on this tirade, but in another thirty seconds he'd have killed her. He was so large he could probably lift the back end of a car alone. There were knife scars along his cheek where somebody had tried to find his throat.

Toby went to the door. "Come outside. Go down the hall and into the next room. There's a light on the wall to your right. Turn it on as you go in. Sit down in a chair."

Sonny kept looking at him with that dead hard expression. He shook himself out of it as Toby backed out of the room and down the hall. Sonny came out, glancing to see him, and moved sluggishly down the hall. The light in Toby's room came on. Toby stayed close to the far wall as he peered into the room. The nigger was sitting in a chair as he had told him to do. Toby slipped back and got the baseball bat and stuck it under his arm.

He entered his room and pulled the other chair all the way across, allowing as much distance between them as possible. He held the pistol on Sonny's chest. Sonny just sat and looked at him, waiting.

"You got your money?"

Sonny did not answer. Toby had seen him take it from the floor.

"Now listen, Sonny . . ." There was a small change in Sonny's face when he realized Toby had recognized him. "How long you been out?"

Sonny acted like he wasn't going to answer. Toby waited a reasonable time.

"All right . . . how long?"

"Today."

"You got out today?"

Sonny ran his hand over his mouth and looked sullenly at the ceiling.

"Well, you sure as God were trying to get back in jail right fast."

Sonny glanced at him, then returned his gaze to the ceiling.

"What did she do?"

Sonny shrugged.

"Listen, Sonny . . . if you had killed that girl, you'd have been gone forever this time. Do you know that?"

No response. The eyes remained on the ceiling, interested in something up there, blinking slowly.

"You got your money. She won't say anything, so you're out of it. Now I want you to listen. You've had too much to drink and somebody made you mad—maybe she did, maybe somebody else—but tomorrow when you wake up you remember that all Toby wanted to do was cool it. I did you a favor tonight. Try to think about that tomorrow."

The large head turned curiously.

"I could have killed you in there. The way you beat that girl . . . going to help her . . . you can see it, can't you?"

He heard sounds on the stairway and he hoped to God she'd had sense enough not to call the police. Sonny would never forget this. It would play in his mind forever and the only way to water it down was to try to make him think about what else could have happened.

"I've got no reason to kill you. You don't even know the girl. You've got no real reason to kill her. So we forget it. It's all over and nobody loses. Right?"

Sonny just looked at him, blinking slowly.

Levi hurried along the hall from the stairway and came immediately to the door. Roxie had gone to him at the cab stand down the street. Sonny let his eyes slide to Levi.

"I heard it was you," Levi said. "What you want to cause trouble for anyway?"

"Take the bat, Levi," Toby said.

He felt the bat slide across his leg. Toby took the pistol in both hands then and snapped it open. He removed the cartridges, twenty-two hollow points, the kind that entered the body making a little hole and came out the size of a silver dollar. He put the cartridges in his pocket.

"Here you go." He tossed the pistol across the room and Sonny caught it in his big hands. "Nobody loses," Toby said. "Okay," he jerked his head toward the door.

Sonny got up, taking his time, looking Toby in the eye all the way to the door. Then he went on out and they heard his heavy step on the stairs.

Toby felt himself go limp then. He was bathed in sweat and his hands shook terribly when he tried to light a cigarette. It felt like somebody was squeezing his heart.

"Roxie come for me," Levi said. "He beat the shit out of her."

"He was about to kill her. Where is she?"

"In the cab."

"Will you go send her back up?"

"Yeah." Levi started off.

"Levi . . . leave the bat."

He took it from Levi and tossed it on the bed. Jesus God, he needed a drink. He thought he'd go down to the bar and catch two or three beers to settle it down inside him. He never wanted one so bad, at least as long as he could remember. He went to the orange crate and took another pill, drinking it down, and sat on the bed. The cigarette was growing warm near his fingers by the time she got back upstairs. She came into the room looking pitiful. Her face was swollen all out of shape. She was going to look bad for two weeks. She sat down in the chair and let her head hang, leaning forward so the hair fell over her face.

"It's all right now," he said.

"He was killing me."

"Why?"

She shook her head. "I don't know. I was nice to him. But he had some kind of trouble. He couldn't get with it and he said something about me messing him up and I figured he was just drunk. I didn't know who he was. Levi told me. And then he started blaming me. I was trying all I could but he kept blaming me for his trouble and then he hit me and I started to scream, but that hand came down on my throat and it never got out. It was getting black . . . all over, Toby, when you came in there."

Toby went to the sink and found a cloth. He moistened it with cool water and raised her head and touched the coolness to her swollen cheek. She closed her eyes and in a moment her body began to shake, coming from inside, but there was no sound at her mouth, just that silent sobbing. He held her against him, wondering if it might not have been smarter to kill him. Sonny wasn't going to forget. He wasn't going to be loose very long, not with the way his head was working, and maybe he'd get in trouble someplace else but God knew Sonny wasn't going to forget.

Roxie gradually became calm. Toby got one of his pills and handed it to her. She didn't ask about it. She got some water from the sink and took it. He pointed to the bed.

"Go to bed. Forget about it now. It's all over." He pulled back the sheet and she removed her robe, still naked, and crawled onto the mattress.

"I thought I was dead," she said.

"If he hadn't hit you, you would have been," he said. "I heard that."

She shook her head and he was afraid she might cry again. He turned out the light and closed the door, locking it.

"Now nothing can hurt you. He'll forget about it in the morning."

"I hurt all over."

"The pill will take care of that."

Toby lay beside her, still dressed, until perhaps half an hour later the pill hit her good and she began to sleep. He got up and sat in the chair and lighted a cigarette, seeing her by the light from the alley. When his eyes grew heavy from the pills, he removed his shirt and trousers and crawled in beside her. She made a sound but did not awaken.

And he wondered where Sonny was. Wondered what was going through his mind, creeping along through that sluggish brain, that near-fool intelligence, whether he had found the box of cartridges already and had slipped six of them into the pistol. He tried to shrug the thought away. So it happened. It couldn't have happened any other way. Except maybe he should have killed him.

10

Levi eased the battered cab into the gravel lot, checking the temperature gauge because he had a small leak in the water pump which he had neglected to replace and the car had a tendency to heat. He turned off the motor and pushed his cap back on his head, sweating profusely at eleven in the morning but attributing part of that to Toby. He opened the door of the cab and waddled to the stand, a small frame building not much bigger than a WPA outhouse, and asked the girl if he'd had any calls. When she told him he had not, he jerked his thumb toward the bar across the street.

"I'll be over there for a few minutes." He wiped his cheek on his sleeve and jaywalked his way to the bar. Roxie was sitting on a stool smoking a cigarette, the bruises on her face still apparent but fading after ten days so that she was back at work when she felt like it. She had her skirt heisted to the limit and was jiggling a leg as she smoked and toyed with a glass of beer some dum-dum had paid for.

"Hey, Levi," she said as he approached.

"You busy?" Levi asked.

She looked around her. Only the hardcore were in the place at eleven in the morning, the shaky ones getting down a few beers before their heads unscrewed and three girls who figured some guy might show up for a matinee. Levi turned and heard her slide from the stool to follow him. He went up the block toward the railroad tracks, turned into the doorway, and climbed the stairs with her beside him.

"What's this about?" she asked.

"Toby," he said.

"What about Toby?" A different tone.

When they reached the top of the stairs, she went ahead, opened her door, and turned on the fan.

"He's hiding now. If the police come, you don't know nothing."

"Oh, Christ," she said. "What'd he do?"

"Well," Levi began, "I'll tell you the whole thing. It was early this morning, eight-thirty or something, and nothing was going on. I'd hauled all the maids I had lined up to work and so I parked the cab and came over. Toby was sitting at his desk and we talked a little bit. He's different, Roxie . . . something's different lately."

"He's sick," she said.

"What with?"

"I don't know. But he's got them pills and . . . I can tell. And he's not drinking anything because he's scared of something."

"He is now," Levi said softly.

She raised her eyebrow and reached for a cigarette which she slid between her lips. "Tell me."

"Yeah. So we was about to go get a cup of coffee when this Assyrian come in. You know, this guy over on Mount Olive Street got the hot dog place . . . and dirty magazines, all that stuff?"

"I know the place."

"He comes in Toby's shop. So Toby turns and he looks at this Assyrian and the guy is standin' there like with his thumbs down in his belt, a big diamond ring on his finger, all that curly hair falling around his head. He smiles real big and says hey to Toby and comes over and squeezes Toby's shoulder, only Toby, he don't say nothing. He don't even look at the guy. So the Assyrian says something about he can't make a living sitting on his ass and laughing big, you know, and then he figures Toby's not funning it up much this morning so he says he's got a job for Toby. So Toby leans over and flips open his book and runs his finger down the figures and it stops and he says, 'You owe me ten dollars.'

"The Assyrian says he don't remember that and Toby says from the last signs he painted, he didn't get paid, and the Assyrian asks did Toby send him a bill, and Toby says he don't send bills and the guy waves his big hand and says, no wonder, he only pays when he gets a bill, but Toby says he come by the place a half a dozen times and he either got the first-of-the-month garbage or the Assyrian was gone."

Levi got up and pulled his chair closer to the fan while Roxie curled up on the bed, taking it in. He lifted his arms to let the air flow around the large circles of sweat on his shirt.

"So," he continued, "the Assyrian waved that off and tells Toby he got another sign he wants painted and he gives Toby this paper. It says DOGS—15¢ and it's got a picture above. It's a hot dog in a bun with the weenie sticking out the end with chili showing and everything. He says, 'I want it almost all the way across the window. Seven feet . . . great big weenie in a bun. Can you do that, Toby?'

"Toby says it will be awful but the Assyrian says on Greasy Corner he sells hot dogs and he makes good money off the dogs, so he's pushing them. Them weenies he uses is mostly cereal and the chili is so watered it runs like piss . . ."

"Levi, what the hell happened?"

"Well, Toby says if the Assyrian will pay him the back bill and another ten he'll do the sign and the guy says sure and if he's gone the girl at the counter will give him the money. So Toby gets all his stuff ready and since I ain't doin' nothin' I say maybe I'll go along and Toby says sure.

"Well, Toby gets to the place and all these clowns are sittin' around chomping on them hot dogs at the counter and this white stringy-haired waitress is running the place. Toby, he goes around the counter and climbs in the window and washes it clean first because it's got so much grease stuck to it, and then he draws the weenie and the bun and the words down below. Then he gets out his paint and I'm havin' a Coke and the stringy-haired girl is acting sassy, like she don't like a black man foolin' around behind the counter, but you know how that rolls off Toby's back . . . he don't pay no attention . . . he just paints that sign. He does it pretty fast . . . big red weenie sticking out of the bun, just like the Assyrian said. So maybe an hour is gone and people are sittin' around watchin' and some are watchin' from outside for a few minutes. So anyway in about an hour Toby gets finished and climbs out of the window and looks at it. The Assyrian is gone, so he hands this stringy-haired bitch the bill with the ten dollars on it the Assyrian never paid, and she looks at him like he's out of his tree. He says the Assyrian told him he'd pay or she'd give him the money, and she slams her hand on her hip and says he didn't tell her *nothin'* about giving no money out of the register and she ain't about to pay him unless Mr. Shadid tells her.

"So Toby stands there and you can see the mad come to his eyes, like he knows he's been had again. Only it ain't like the old Toby . . . like maybe he used to figure he'd finally collar the Assyrian and dig the money out of him . . . not the way Toby is now, because he's sober and . . . I don't know, anyway different, and the look in his eyes is no look like you'd want Toby to have and he asks very soft . . . where's he gone? And she says for Christ's sake she don't know where he's gone. She ain't got no leash on him and she don't like talking to a mad nigger, and maybe a little afraid anyway, so she just turns her back and walks off, all those guys still chomping on them hot dogs, and Toby looks around and he shakes his head slow and then he done it."

"He done what?" she asked.

"Well . . . nobody had any idea that Toby was goin' to do nothin' but he turns around and he looks at the sign and his shoulders are all tight, like another Toby, and he looks at the sign for a minute and I'm thinking he's gonna throw a pickle jar through it but he don't. He goes back very slow and he opens his paint stuff and he climbs back in the window and he gets all the stuff ready and then, it's like he goes crazy, the way his hands move, so fast you wouldn't believe it. This paint dries quick . . . it's some kind of fast stuff he uses, and nobody knows what he's doin' but it's clear he ain't just smearing the sign. Something is in his head and we all watch and a few people on the outside watch and pretty soon this thing begins to look like something. In another five minutes he's done. The waitress is standin' there with her mouth open and all the guys at the counter puts down their hot dogs and just stares and Toby climbs out of the window and he looks at the sign and he kind of jerks his head, satisfied, and packs his case and comes around the counter. I never seen nothin' like it."

"What did he paint?" Roxie asked, leaning forward.

"Well, what he done . . . he changed that hot dog and the bun to a great big hard prick. You ain't never seen nothin' like it . . . it don't look like nothin' else by then but a hard dick seven feet long. I mean, if you blowed up a picture of a real one, it couldn't look no more like it."

"Jesus God," she said.

"So he come around the counter, don't say a word to no-body, and he grabs me by the shirt and we get the hell out of there. He's making this sound in his throat, like he's laughing but it's not quite the same, and he's walking with jerky steps . . . like he's had all he can take and that's it. He goes across the street to that beer joint and puts his case down and climbs on the stool by the window and looks out across at the sign and just ås calm as anything he turns to the guy and says he'd like a tall-boy can of beer. And with the steadiest hand I ever seen he pours it and takes a long slow sip and his eyes get soft and his shoulders go loose and he turns on the stool to look out across the street. Well, how many times you ever seen a seven-foot sign of a hard-on?"

Roxie shook her head, a small smile at her lips.

"Well, this waitress . . . in a minute she come runnin' out to go next door to make a call and them men are startin' to stop on the street, like maybe ten or so, and they are pointin' at the sign and slappin' each other on the back and havin' a good time, and then this lady walks by and she looks to see what the hell and she sees the sign and from across the street you can see she turns red as hell and jerks her head straight down the sidewalk and nearly runs.

"Then the cars goin' down the street see the thing . . . you know, the people all standin' there pointin' like that, so they look and one guy puts on his brakes when he sees the prick and the guy comin' behind him looks too but he don't see the other guy put on the brakes, so he rams right into the back end of the car . . . they get out and look at the headlights smashed all over the street and the radiator losing all the water, and the waitress comes out of next door and goes back in the place. She gets a rag but it's been a while and the paint is almost hard so she can't do anything but smear just a little bit and that don't even spoil the prick. So she gives that up because she's too shook to be foolin' with the sign anyway.

"Well, if you really want a cop in this town it takes forever sometimes and that was what happened to them two guys in the wreck. All the traffic is backing up behind them and there's a lot of honking so that when the cop finally gets there he has to walk a block because of the traffic. He don't notice the sign . . . thinking about the wreck . . . and Toby finishes his beer and orders another one and he's beginning to enjoy it, you know, and the bartender gives him the beer and we all sit there and watch. Pretty soon the waitress is out there pointin' at the sign and the cop looks at it and then he looks back again like he don't believe it the first time. So his molars practically fall out and he goes back to the squad car down the street and talks into the radio. About then the Assyrian comes racing along the sidewalk because the waitress has got hold of him and he looks at the sign and grabs a handful of his curly hair and bends over, red in the face, and starts jumpin' up and down like one of them Indian rain dancers.

"Toby likes that. He takes a good sip of beer and chuckles real big. Pretty soon there must be sixty people around, some of them gettin' out of the cars and comin' down to see what it's all about . . . and the Assyrian runs in and tries to wash the sign off but it's dry by now . . . and he tries a razor blade but that is slow goin' and so he comes back out . . . and you can tell he's talkin' about Toby, pointin' down across the tracks, and I say, 'Uh-oh,' but Toby just puts his hand on my shoulder and keeps watching. In a minute a couple of plainclothes detectives come and they look at the sign and then look at each other and kind of grin a little— you never seen nothin' like it in your life.

"The cops start to clear the cars out and they write up the wreck and the cops tell people to move on but more people are showing up as the word gets up in the other blocks and they can't do much, so they send for another car. After maybe twenty-five . . . thirty minutes from the time we leave, the Assyrian gets a ladder and comes outside and has some sheet material which he nails to the wood above the window so it drapes down over that picture. Then he climbs down and nails it at the bottom and shakes his fist. So when they can't see anymore, the people start goin' in the hot dog place to see it from the inside, and the cop tells him he's got to cover it all up probably. Anyway Toby finishes his beer and he gets off the stool and he's like the old Toby. He got no troubles. And he picks up his case and starts to the door and I say where in the hell does he think he's goin' and he says back to the shop and I tell him they will be lookin' for him and he can't go back there. So he figures I'm right. I tell him to go out the back door of the bar and wait . . . I will come down the alley to pick him up in the cab. I leave him behind and go get the cab and there he is, standin' out in the alley with his case. He gets in and says he's figured it out and he don't want to go to jail . . . he says something about obscenity code or something. And so he tells me to take him to the liquor store. He buys two quarts and comes back out. Then he tells me to take him over to that bad house on River Bridge Street. I drive him over there and he gets out and tells me to come get him when they stop lookin' for him. So he goes in that place . . . the big two-story white place . . ."

"I don't know it," she said. She did not seem too happy with Toby in the bad house.

"Anyway I come back here and park the cab. So if anybody's lookin' for Toby, you don't know nothin'."

Roxie leaned back on the bed and crossed her leg up high and he could see she wasn't wearing no underwear. She grinned. "That's my man," she said almost proudly.

"The Assyrian, I guess he don't know what to do. He's got to hire somebody to scrape all that paint off and that won't be easy with a razor blade . . ."

Roxie laughed and covered her mouth with her hand. In a moment her face changed. "He gonna get drunk?" she said.

"Well . . . that won't be nothin' new."

"But maybe he's too sick."

Levi frowned. He had seen Toby drunk so many times over the years that he couldn't see much harm in it.

"And he'll get feisty when he gets drunk. They got women in that bad house?"

Levi nodded to her. "A few hang around," he said.

Her mouth got hard and her eyes narrowed. "I don't like it," she said evenly.

"Hell, Roxie . . . he can't come back here. They lookin' for him everyplace. The Assyrian wants him in jail."

"Well, by God, I'd rather have him in jail than in bed with one of them nigger bitches with the clap."

"He ain't gonna do that," Levi said without a great deal of conviction.

"That," she said sliding from the bed, "we gonna see about."

In an hour she was bathed and dressed. She went down the stairs and crossed the street to where Levi was sitting in the office.

"Take me down there," she said.

Levi's moon face looked up from a copy of a Negro girlie magazine which he placed on the desk. He took a pen and marked the page by closing the magazine with the pen inside. "If you go down there and make trouble, it's bad for everybody."

"I'm not gonna make no trouble," she said.

She followed him to the cab and climbed in beside him.

"He's just there with a couple bottles. What you so worried about?"

"I don't like it."

She looked at the houses, stately, well kept, but as the cab traveled along the street she could see how they had begun to go down, needing a coat of paint, repair of a shutter, the grass needing mowing, the white people trying to sell, trying to get away from the advancing Negro settlement. The cab crossed an intersection and suddenly all the kids outside, the people on the porches were black. There was a little girl in pigtails sitting in a swing, a long rope from the tree limb attached to an old tire. She pushed with one foot to keep herself moving, looking up into the rays of sunlight that crept through the leaves. On down the street Roxie saw an old man with a cane coming along slowly, sliding his feet, dressed in what was surely his best suit, and she wondered where he was going. The cab pulled over to the curb.

"I'll go with you," Levi said, but Roxie knew he was only going to warn Toby, and she wanted to see what the hell he was doing up there.

"No, you go on back."

Levi rubbed his hand across the ample flesh of his face. "Roxie, has Toby ever said anything about those guys you take up to your room for money?"

"No." She had the door partly open.

"If I was you, I don't think I'd go in there."

"I'm goin'."

"Well . . . if I got in there and saw somethin' I didn't like . . . I believe I'd just keep my mouth shut and come back out and forget it. You better not try to own Toby. Nobody owns Toby."

She considered that, listening to the passing traffic.

"Let's go back," Levi said.

She got out of the car and closed the door. "I'll be back later if anybody wants me," she said.

She walked quickly up the walk, fearing what she might see up there, growing angry already . . . and yet what Levi said . . . she knew she couldn't push it too far. It was a large white house but needing paint like the others. Big place with lots of rooms. Once it had been considered fashionable. She rapped on the door but nothing happened. After a few minutes she opened the screen and went inside. There was a dark hallway, bare floor, which led into a large room. There was nobody around. In the distance she heard voices so she followed the sound to the left into another room. There was a table around which sat four men, two of them bare above the waist because of the heat. There were cards on the table . . . and money. The men on the opposite side of the table looked up and one of them, a big lean buck, grinned and raised his eyebrows, a little drunk she thought. "Hey, baby . . . how you?" he said.

"Where's Toby Snow?" she asked.

They looked at each other.

"You a friend of his?"

"You bet your sweet ass I am. Now where is he?"

One of the men looked at his cards, holding them tightly in his hand. "Upstairs," he said.

She turned around, feeling their eyes on her as she left the room.

"Yeah, man," somebody said.

She climbed the stairs. Apparently there wasn't much going on at noon. These were mostly night people, except for the gamblers who seemed to live their lives holding the cards. Upstairs there were doors down the hallway, most of them closed. It occurred to her she could make somebody mad as hell if she started opening doors to find . . . she didn't know what, but she had a good idea. She hesitated outside the first door and listened but heard nothing. She went to the next and heard voices, a couple girls, and she went on. At the third door she paused and heard a woman talking and then she heard Toby laugh. *The goddam bastard.* She turned the knob and found that the door wasn't locked so she threw it open.

They looked up as she stood in the doorway, and she never felt quite so relieved in her life, though she wasn't sure what she might have found if she'd arrived an hour later or maybe a half hour before. He was lying on the bed with a bottle between his legs, fully dressed and looking a little silly, a little high, and the girl sat on the bed with one foot on the floor, the other crossed at the knee, wearing one of those go-go skirts that came up to there, and no top, just a brassiere.

Toby looked at her and smiled. "Hey, sweetpot," he said.

The nigger girl turned around and Roxie could see she didn't have very good tits and her hair was sticky with that mess they used to keep it straight and she had a flattened nose, ugly as hell. The girl looked at her very suspiciously, especially that purse Roxie carried, and Roxie smiled at that because she knew the girl was afraid she'd get into that purse, coming up here after her man, and find a knife. She walked across the room, swinging the purse, taking nice strides as the skirt hugged her thighs, and the girl took that in as she got up to face her.

"Honey, I believe you can go now," Roxie said.

The girl glanced at Toby, but not in question because she was sure God leaving. She left plenty of space as she passed and Roxie heard the door close behind her.

"Well, baby," she said. "You got yourself in one mess."

He smiled. "Did you see it?"

"No . . . Levi told me about it."

He smiled foolishly, reaching down between his legs and

taking the bottle by the neck. He opened it, took one small sip, and screwed the cap back on.

"Well," he said, "it was nice."

"Maybe two years nice if they catch you."

She saw his face grow sober for an instant. "Two years?"

"I called Julius. He got out his law book and read it to me. Obscenity. It's a misdemeanor, whatever that is, to paint a sign like that. You go to court and if they get you, you catch maybe two years or a two-thousand-dollar fine, or both. Did you have that much fun?"

He waved it away. "Aw, hell, Roxie . . . it didn't do any harm." He let his eyes drift to the ceiling and then he frowned. "Two years. That seems right steep."

She sat on the edge of the bed and crossed her legs. Reaching into the purse, she took out two cigarettes, got them both going, and handed one to Toby. He took it and shook his head.

"I didn't know that," he said.

"Well, they just don't let any son of a bitch go around painting a big tool on the goddam window. And Levi said the Assyrian was after you."

"He wouldn't pay me. He thought he could get around me like he did before."

"That may be the case, but the police don't give a damn about what he did with his bill. They just saw that thing hanging out . . ."

"It wasn't hanging."

She suppressed a smile. "No, Toby wouldn't paint it hanging. He'd have it in full glory." She took the bottle out of his hand and took a short drink. It turned her stomach. "God, that's awful." She pulled hard on the cigarette. When she was able, she turned back to him. He was looking at the ceiling again. "You aren't supposed to drink anymore," she said.

"Who says that?"

"Somebody . . . the doctor. You had them pills."

He shrugged.

"Are you sick, Toby?"

The eyes came down from the ceiling and leveled on her, gentle . . . easy. "I feel pretty good," he said.

She shook her head. "We better get you out of town. For a while. Maybe they'll forget it after a while."

"No," he said.

"They could give you two *years*, Toby," she said.

He shook his head. "I'm not going anyplace. I'm going to stay right here and drink a little whiskey and when I get done, I'll come back and nothing will happen."

"You're crazy."

"No."

"I got some money. We could go to Charlotte and raise a little hell for a while. When Levi says it's quiet, we can come back."

"No."

"All right!" She was losing patience. He acted like he *wanted* to go to jail. "I'll get us a place . . . at night Levi will sneak you out to a place I rent and we can stay there for a while . . . here in town."

"No."

"You gonna stay right here?"

"A day or two. I plan to drink a little whiskey."

Roxie moistened her lips and told herself to go easy. "I don't like them girls. They all got the clap. You *know* that."

His hand came to rest on hers. "Don't worry about that. I don't have any interest in that."

She cut her eyes to him. Hell, did he think she didn't know better than that? "That bitch was in here trying to get your ass when I got here."

"Well . . . she didn't."

"She might have." Then she became afraid that she'd pushed him too much. A feeling of fear was in her stomach, but when she looked back at him he was reading the label on the bottle. "All right," she said, "but if you want that tool handled, you let me do it. If there's any to be had, I want it."

He nodded.

Roxie got up and went to the door, aware that he was watching her. She did not turn back toward him. "Toby."

"Yeah."

"If you cut one of them girls, you wash off good with alcohol and pee right after."

There was no response. She had to turn around. She didn't want to, but she had to see. He had pulled up in bed, almost sitting up, looking at her the way he did, amused at her in a way, and it was all she could do to keep from going over there and throwing herself on him. He smiled.

"Shit," she said softly.

She closed the door and hurried along the hallway.

11

The shade was drawn but a small breeze occasionally pushed it inside, allowing a narrow stream of bright light to fall across his face. The sudden brightness was as unpredictable as the breeze, coming and going abruptly. Toby lay with his eyes closed, waiting, dreading the light. His head was throbbing. Faces appeared on his eyelids, faces he had never seen before, a thing he found incredible. The faces undoubtedly were a product of his mind . . . his brain cells, through some process he could not understand and affected by the quantity of alcohol, contrived to project the images so that he could see them with his eyes closed. They moved, turning toward him . . . a fat man, black, smiling like the devil himself, the expression on his face cynical . . . *We got you, baby*. Toby studied the face carefully. He tried to think of all the faces he'd ever seen, the show business personalities, the friends, the famous . . . but this face was different and he wondered again how his mind could possibly create a strange face. Soon the light would come through the window and destroy the image, yet he waited apprehensively for the next face,

wondering if there might be some clue to these manifesta-
tions. And another came, a woman who shook her head
slowly and, with that much alcohol in his body, he pondered
the possibility that these people were dead, that this was
truly real, and that in his state he was being tortured or
privileged to see those who had gone before. They were all
disapproving somehow, some amused at his condition, some
perhaps sad. "Who are you?" he asked the face on his eyelids. It was a man, tall, angular, bald and black, and he was
frowning, his lips compressed. The face turned slightly when
he spoke, the head inclined toward him as though the face
knew he had spoken but had not heard. "I said who are
you?" Now the face had little expression, just staring at him.
"Go away," Toby said. The face did not retreat. He tried to
watch the eyes, dark, solemn eyes, and he discovered that
the eyes did not blink, and he was certain that this man
must be among the dead . . . like the body of the man in the
hospital morgue, staring as though seeing inside of him.

The shade sailed on the breeze and the face was gone in
the light but this time it returned when the light had vanished.

"Listen here . . . what do you want?" he shouted.

He heard a sound at the door, heard footsteps, but did
not open his eyes out of a ghastly fear that the man had
entered and was standing at the foot of the bed.

"Who you talkin' to, Toby?"

It was the girl. He started to speak but coughed, a wrack-
ing sound that only invited other spasms. When they passed,
he lay exhausted against the pillow. He reached out sight-
lessly to feel for the bottle. His head was killing him. "Is
there any left?" he asked.

"A little. Toby . . . you had enough. You don't look so
good."

He ignored that. It seemed there was no stopping, that if

he stopped sending the balm to his nerves, which now was almost ineffective, he would explode, just break inside. He took a small drink. He didn't know how much he had had; somehow the number of bottles had escaped him. He did recall sending out for more, but he couldn't seem to remember when he had done that, today, yesterday. . . . He was hurting because he hadn't had anything to drink for quite a while, but that period he couldn't remember either . . . a month perhaps, maybe less, and his system had changed, not drinking it every day, and when he went back to the pattern he had known so well, the liquor had a greater impact, bringing the faces to his eyelids.

"Who was you talkin' to?" she asked again.

He ran his tongue over his lips. The faces did not come when she was in the room . . . if she was really there.

"I don't know," he said. His voice cracked as he spoke and he could not seem to control it.

"Toby, you got to quit," she said.

He did not reply and did not hear her leave. He waited for a while, thinking she would speak, and when she did not he was not certain she had ever been there at all.

No faces came, at least not immediately. He tried to make images of real people, some of whom he would like to see again, to talk to for a little while. Why did the faces have to be strangers? But he had not created those faces. They had come of their own accord. Sal . . . he wished her face would come. He tried to make it appear but what came was not alive at all. It was only the memory of a snapshot he had taken of her in the yard by the house, standing there with Danny's hand in hers . . . two or three then, he was, in short pants, squinting his eyes against the sunlight so that in the photograph he looked angry. But Sal was smiling . . . during the happy years, or at least years that he had thought were happy.

I made a mess of it, Sal. I did the best I could but . . . I don't know. Somehow I never had enough in me to do it right. He was a good boy . . . you'd have been proud of him, but I figured later maybe I could have changed it. If I'd taught him something else, he might not have gone like he did. Maybe he couldn't tell me . . . it could be that he was wanting to get away from me. I thought we had a good thing . . . it seemed like it. I just don't know . . . I don't know anymore. It's all gone out of focus, like it was with us. I remember the good times and I could never figure why you left me. And the next thought was good-by . . . he was telling her good-by but in a way that meant something he did not want in his mind, so he stopped that thought an instant after it had already made itself known and erased it. No.

An image of his father appeared at his command. The only image that seemed appropriate, the one he always remembered, was that of his father sitting in church with that heavy suit on, the black one he wore even in summer and the tall starched collar that seemed to squeeze his neck so that he could not move comfortably, like a plaster of Paris cast . . . sitting stiffly in the church pew, ramrod straight, his jaws closed tightly together, his eyes fierce as he clutched the Bible and listened to the preacher. He could remember that stern face admonishing him for having what the kids called *fun* . . . it was a bad word. The reward was in the next life with Jesus. Everything that a man did went down in a book and one day he had to stand before God while they tallied it all up and balanced it on a gold scale and if he had not done well, if he had had *fun,* if he had not been humble before God, if he had not walked the straight and narrow, he would go to Hell and endure indescribable suffering forever and ever.

He could not remember feeling his father's hand on his

shoulder, never a caress, a really gentle word, except perhaps the words he said when Toby got back from the war and was in the hospital with his wound and they came to visit him. His father had stood stiffly at the end of the bed and, while his mother talked away, his father said nothing. When it was nearly time for them to go, his father, appearing uncomfortable, told him that if he had suffered, it was God's will, that God was trying to teach him something. And then it came. He said the captain had written them a letter telling how he had been courageous in battle and he said falteringly that he was proud of that, that God had used him, had given him the courage to do his task. Then he turned, his hat in his hand, and set his jaw and was silent again. There was nothing more to say. But, like a note of music, the tone had been slightly different for a brief moment, not quite but almost gentle the only time he could remember.

When he was discharged he came home, what was then home, for a visit before he went to college on the G.I. Bill. His father said a grace at the table that lasted longer than the meal. There was little conversation. It was as though the old man saw through him, that he knew he still had that itch for fun, that he had not given his life to earning a place in the next one.

He saw some of the boys that night. They rode around for a time, drinking some cheap wine, and he came in stumbling. His father got up and saw him. He stood before him, those black feet protruding from the long nightshirt.

"I will not have a drunkard in my house," he said.

Toby's tie was askew, his hair uncombed. He looked up into the iron face and said, "Papa . . . a man can be drunk on a lot of things. I found that out."

The old man returned to his bedroom and the next day Toby left. He did not return until he went back to the

funeral, because his mother insisted, and found, as he suspected, that the face in the casket was no different in death
from the way it had been for most of his life . . . stony, rigid.

Toby brushed the old man out of his mind. He remembered the college days, good days. He read like lightning
and found that it was not difficult, the studying. There was
time for pleasure too. He worked in the college cafeteria
washing pots and pans, sometimes humming a tune . . . and
taken with the dark girl who worked out in the dining area,
washing the tables off with a rag, sweeping the floor when
the meals were over. He'd had women before, on those par-
ties in the army, even a couple of white women in Europe,
but it never meant anything special and either they felt self-
conscious or maybe they just didn't feel the things he felt
. . . he didn't know, but he'd found it a not particularly satis-
fying experience. Maybe they had to have that down in the
record, an accomplishment—I slept with a black man—a kind
of measure of all past and perhaps future experiences.

He was a junior student and the girl, not particularly
pretty and rather quiet, sometimes stared at him for long
moments as he laughed and carried on with all that grab-ass
nonsense back in the kitchen, and sometimes he'd see her
smile slightly. He met her leaving one evening and walked
her to her dormitory. No, not very pretty really, but never-
theless captivating. He had asked her to a dance . . . and
there was a wild thing afterward. Somebody had a place to
go shack up and they went there with the others, hitting the
bottle pretty good, most of them, though the girl took just
one drink the whole night and the rest of the time she held
onto his arm while he frolicked. He didn't get her that night.
The passion came like a storm, and for a while she was lost
in it but managed to shift positions at the right moment so
that he failed, and she was angry with him the next day, but
he didn't worry about that . . . it would pass.

Two or three weeks later he got her in the back seat of a car parked behind the dormitory. He just walked over and opened the door of a car and told her to get in and the instant she put her foot inside that car she was gone. For a time he deceived himself into thinking he had done it, but later, when he'd sit and look at her, not speaking for long periods, he came to realize that she had made up her mind before she ever got in that car. She gave it to him and he was never sure why. He hadn't intended the affair to go beyond that but somehow, like clouds gathering on a summer afternoon, it got bigger and bigger with time. He couldn't remember ever asking her to marry him, but he gave her a ring and when he graduated they set a date and it just happened.

And what went wrong after that, after the child, or when it started, he didn't know, but if he was going to die now he felt that it was wrong not to know, at least, that it was an injustice not to know, that his father's God was pulling a fast one by leaving him nothing but the note that he had destroyed long ago so that the boy might never stumble across it.

After he gave up hoping she would ever come back, there was the boy . . . he visualized him in his uniform, the final product going off to a kind of world he had once known and for the most part had managed to forget. But he had planned it differently this time. A lawyer . . . with dignity and poise to match his mind, that was the thing. Maybe the boy had been trying to tell him he didn't want that. Maybe he was wrong in thinking he understood the boy and what was right for him. And then they brought his body back and that was all. It was everything. Sal . . . then the boy. And he didn't blame God because it would make more sense to blame a roulette wheel, a throw of the dice. It just happened.

What became of the rest of it? Gone. Like the level of liquid in his bottle, not noticeably lower at first but suddenly very near the bottom, alarmingly so, before he realized it. The trips to the jail to sleep it off, never resisting, never belligerent, as though it didn't matter, even when he felt terrible and contemplated a rather bad morning, at which time he went before the city judge and listened to the officer —he knew most of them well by then—telling how they found him down on all fours searching for the bridge from his mouth, which, for whatever reason, had got lost . . . or just standing, weaving, on the main street, looking into the brightly lighted windows . . . and the judge looked down from the bench and asked if he was guilty or not guilty, a formality they went through that was hardly worth the effort because he always reported himself guilty, at which time the judge would give him the sentence, ten days or ten dollars, which sometimes he paid and sometimes not. He'd be led into the jail and, after they brought him some food and he ate, despite the bad smell in the place, he'd tell the jailer he wanted something to do to pass the time, and they'd give him a broom or a mop and a bucket and he'd set out to clean up the prison, humming away. They brought him books and on one occasion, when the World Series was in progress, they let him out of the cell to watch the game on television, a portable set one of the officers had brought to the station. How many times? He could not remember. Sometimes, if it was late and nobody saw him on the street, the officer would put him in the squad car and drive him home because there really wasn't any reason to lock Toby up, a waste of his time and theirs.

Later he moved to the room above the sign shop because it was too far to walk and he didn't like to pay a cab. He'd owned only one car in his life. He was always afraid he might drive when he was drunk and do something terrible.

Roxie was there when he moved in, with all those young studs racing around her trying to get a good sniff like so many dogs chasing a bitch in heat. Toby had not participated in that activity and he thought that it bothered her some, that he didn't try her, so she got to running around upstairs in a pair of hip-huggers and a brassiere, a low-cut one that seemed to expose all but the nipples, pausing to lean at his door, provocative . . . Hey, how you doin'? *Yeah*. And he'd take a sip and offer her one, which most often she refused.

He was in the bar one evening pouring a little liquor into a glass of beer when she strolled in looking like a black statue, wearing the low-cut white dress with the high-hemmed skirt. He looked at her and turned back to his drink, feeling her slide onto the stool beside him. "Hey, neighbor," she said.

He took out a cigarette and lighted it, exhaling and taking it from his lips, and felt her slide it from his fingers and when he looked, she glared at him beneath half-closed lids, a saucy smile, and he took another cigarette from his pocket . . . and that bothered her, that she wasn't having all that much effect.

"Do you do anything but drink?" she asked.

He grinned into his glass. "Occasionally," he said. "I paint signs. If you ever need one, in your business . . ."

Her full mouth narrowed to a line and the eyes grew hard. "So what about my business?"

"Nothing, Roxanne," he said, using her name for the first time. "It's yours to do with and that's fine. I don't ask how much you drink . . . you got a right?"

There was no place for her to go with that. "Well, shit," she said.

She left the bar and threw herself down at a table of near-drunk studs and laughed too loudly and kept looking his way, he noticed in the mirror behind the bar, and he thought for the first time how beautiful she really was.

That night he was lying at the window when she came upstairs. He heard her footsteps on the boards, the heels tapping away, slowing as they reached his door. She stood there silhouetted by the light that came from the alley. "You asleep?" she asked softly.

"No . . ."

"Well . . ." and she waited. When he said nothing, she took the step, as she had to take them all along, one after another. "Can I come in?"

"Yes," he said, lighting a cigarette.

She sat on the edge of the bed. In the dark he could feel her looking at him. "I didn't mean to be ugly at the bar," she said.

He drew on the smoke and turned toward the window and spoke to the night. "You weren't ugly. It just didn't come off like you had planned."

"What do you mean?"

"I said what I meant."

He thought she might leave at that, but she didn't. "I found out about you," she said.

"All right," he said and finished the cigarette, all he wanted of it.

She took it and stepped on it. "Do you know what I found out?"

He turned toward her. "No . . . I have no idea."

"One man said you didn't have a knife . . . didn't have anything . . . that you just walk off. But nobody ever has much to say, tough stuff. A guy said you didn't care if you had any money. That you didn't get uptight about anything. That people felt this thing for you . . . a woman said she'd like to go to bed with you *because* . . . but she couldn't seem to put it into words . . . just a feeling. And they said you just took your little drink and went on, painting those signs until your shoulders got stooped . . . maybe you're crazy?"

He smiled.

"And you don't have a woman? Is something wrong with you?"

"I don't pay for lovemaking," he said. "That's your business. So why act like a damned fool?"

"You think I'm pretty?"

"Beautiful," he said.

"I already know that . . . did you know that?"

He nodded. "A woman knows a lot of things she doesn't feel."

"Well, there you go again. What the hell does that mean?"

He answered patiently. "What it says . . . do you feel beautiful?"

She did not answer for a time. "No," she said.

He turned to the window and lifted the bottle.

"My old man raped me," she said. "I was just a kid—a big kid, but inside I was just a kid."

When he did not answer, she asked him for a drink from the bottle. She made a sound like regurgitation as she took the bottle from her lips. She put it back in his hand and he took a small sip.

"I don't see how you do that," she said.

She must have thought he was falling asleep when he said nothing for so long. He felt her move from the bed, heard the zipper of her dress sing, a brassiere clip tap against the floor, and she was back again, her weight stretched out along the length of the bed. She put her open hand on his chest.

"I want to sleep with you," she said.

He turned his head toward her until he could see the light from the alley on her face. Slowly he took the bottle from the bed and set it on the windowsill, still watching her, and took her in his arms. He could not imagine being a woman, feeling what a woman feels, but he could imagine those young studs hammering away at her with pelvis-breaking strokes. But that was not his way. And a bit drunk as he was, time didn't matter, so a very long, pleasant time passed before he once again lay on his back. He figured she was vivacious, couldn't stand not being wanted that way . . . or maybe just curious. He saw that steady, solemn gaze the following morning near noon when he came into the bar, paint smeared on his shirt, for a quick beer. She was sitting at the table with a couple of young men and he saw the look in the mirror and nodded to her. He thought that either she looked at everybody she'd had that way or something had happened that he didn't understand . . . which was the case, and he was not sure he understood it yet. So for two years she had been his woman and, while the others paid for her, she came to him. Two years, sometimes just lying next to him without any physical contact . . . or talking long into the night. She told the woman down the street to stay away from him. Levi reported that small conversation, which occurred after he'd left the bar, after that girl—he couldn't remember which one—put her arm around him. Yet everyday he expected her to go, to leave him, to find somebody, perhaps because he had been through that once, had lived with a woman, thinking all the time it was right, and suddenly . . . gone. So he waited to answer her need, two times a week to make love, and perhaps just as good, the many hours of quiet talk, a memorable expression, a tone of voice . . . moments caught like pictures in his mind.

The liquor was wearing off. He knew his mind was clearing because those things he had been thinking were real, and yet he remembered seeing those faces of strangers on his eyelids. Somebody in the room too, he thought, though he wasn't sure. The steady throbbing in his head had been growing unbearable. It was rotten whiskey. He took a drink of it and felt his stomach contract. He couldn't drink it and he couldn't face the idea of stopping, because then the shakes would come and he figured it would take a handful of those red pills to cope with them.

He turned the bottle up again and nothing came. He opened his eyes. It was empty. He laid it beside him on the bed and covered his eyes with his arm. Then she was sitting beside him. He hadn't heard her come in but he could tell by her touch before she spoke. He looked at her, his eyes watering, and saw Levi behind her. No sound came as he tried to speak.

"Help me, Levi," she said.

He was up, on the side of the bed, his wrist gripped by her small, strong hands, his arm placed around her shoulder. He felt himself come up with Levi on the other side.

"They said he hasn't eaten. Not since he came here. He looks terrible."

There was a sensation of going down as he took the steps. The sun was gone and the air cool as they stepped outside. He was in the cab, Roxanne sitting beside him as Levi drove.

"Can we get him upstairs, Levi?"

"Yes. We'll make it."

"Nobody should know," she said.

"It's all right."

His head was aching. If he could get some cold water and a couple of red pills, he thought it would help. He closed his eyes and felt the cab moving along the street, the slightest shift of the springs moving his body to one side or the other. The cab stopped and Levi was around there quickly.

"We can make it. Come on, Toby."

He tried to help, stumbling for the steps, and then he felt that mattress, that same old familiar contour against his back. He tried to look at them but they were all blurred. He knew he couldn't talk; there was no point in trying. He closed his eyes, hoping against hope that he could sleep, that when he awoke the throbbing in his head might be gone.

He did not know how long he had been there. It did not seem long, but something had happened to time . . . to the days, the hours . . . the sun. And then, as though from a distance, he heard the voices . . . angry voices.

"We got a call. They said he was on the way here. He's got to go."

"He's sick," Roxie said. "He can't go."

"Move . . ."

"Them sons a bitches at that goddam bad house. Soon as he was gone, they called on him."

"All right, Toby . . . get up. You're going with us."

Suddenly he was on his feet and he'd have fallen if they hadn't held him. His head was clearing now, still painful, but he understood and while he could not see the officers he knew they were taking him in.

When they got downstairs Roxie insisted she would go with them to post bond. "It's all right, baby," she said.

He pushed his thumb and a finger against his eyes until she pulled his hand away. Then they were in the station, holding him upright before they folded him up in a chair. He heard them mention obscenity. Roxie was hanging in there with them, talking about calling Julius and asking how much the bond was, when his arm fell from the chair. He looked at it strangely. He tried to lift it but nothing happened. He could not move the fingers. It was like trying to move another man's fingers. They were arguing in the background and he could not move. His jaw sagged open and he was vaguely aware that something was happening, that somehow his body was failing him. His head fell to the side and it was becoming very difficult to see. He took his right arm as they argued and pulled against the arm of the chair. Then he stiffened his right leg against the floor and pushed himself up, he thought, but he lost the chair. It turned over perhaps, but before everything began to whirl, he could feel the cool tile floor of the station against his cheek.

12

Curtis the Kid made the difference, though Roxie
had never cared much for him—his white ways—
but he came down after they got Toby to the
stairway and, no bigger than he was, got hold of
his body and practically carried him, alone, up the stairs to
the bed. And it was the kid who felt his pulse and listened
to his breathing, knowing more than she or Levi that he was
in pretty bad shape.

He told Roxie to stay with him and turned to Levi in the
dim light of the room and asked him to come, that he was
going to get a doctor, though Levi looked skeptical. Curtis
went out the door and down the stairs like he didn't have a
doubt in the world that Levi would follow.

So she sat beside him and wondered what it was in Toby
that made him do this, like maybe he had to sacrifice himself whenever he saw more of the world than was tolerable
. . . those times he shut it off, turned out all the lights in his
brain, and in that dark alcoholic oblivion, rested, free of
man's capability to hate the way man did. He told her once
. . . he said, "Roxie, do you know the only feeling a man is

allowed to feel openly in our society . . . the only feeling people will accept?"

Since she hadn't known what was going on in his mind, she said no, she didn't. He stared at the burning ember of his cigarette as though the wisdom came from that small light and he said the feeling was rage. When he had wept, as a child, his mama . . . well, she said, "Big boys don't cry," and he was shamed to silence while a little volcano smouldered inside. And every time, Toby said, he needed to feel something beautiful or sad he had to do it privately, in hiding, or people would think him crazy. But let a strange man touch his woman, let a man crumple his automobile fender, and he could get out there and yell his ass off, maybe take a pipe wrench and threaten to bash in a man's head, and everybody understood. He could come home and throw an empty bottle against the wall and curse the boss man, and his wife understood . . . that was all right. But if he sat down with the weight of all his terrible responsibility, finally too much to bear, if he lowered his face and sobbed, she got to wringing her hands in fear that he was maybe falling apart inside.

So a man had no place to go. He couldn't cry, or if he did, he had to hide. Toby understood man, knew why he acted the way he did, but there was not very much place in Toby's life for hate . . . for the rage. So Toby took his drink and seldom got happy, hardly ever got high or elated like the others . . . no yelling *Whooooopee* for Toby . . . but just that easy kind of numbness that most often made his face appear sad.

They came up the stairs noisily, the kid stepping aside at the doorway to let the doctor enter. Roxie watched him feel all over Toby's body, watched him take out the stethoscope and listen to Toby's heart and wrap that cloth around his arm to take his blood pressure. He was a tall man, white, maybe in a hurry to get back to his party. Then he got busy, got to doing the doctor thing, taking out a syringe and filling it with some juice which he stuck in Toby's arm, then another one which he stuck in his other arm. He sat on Toby's old wooden chair with the prescription pad on his knee and kept writing and tearing off pages until he looked like a nigger gambler in a crap game, wadding up those bills while they threw the dice.

He gave a handful of prescriptions to Curtis, explaining each one, and when he turned to leave he looked at her and told her to see that he took the pills like it indicated on the bottles. The kid and Levi went to the drug store to get all that medicine and Roxie sat down in the chair by the bed and listened to him breathe and knew that her man didn't have many of these sprees left in him, that the next one, maybe the one after that, and they would find him gone. She touched his limp arm gently, wondering to herself why she could not be enough, why loving him as she did she couldn't fill that great empty place inside of Toby. And she knew as she felt his flesh that it was none of the things the others worried about, not the white man's world, not the black man's pain down in South Carolina . . . because to Toby there wasn't much of a white man's world or a black man's world. It was just the world. He told her once, *"It's not what's around you, Roxie, not the job, not the big car, the house, or the wife, the kids, or who hates you so much . . . it's all inside. There isn't any geographical cure, no thing anybody can say or do to stop the hurt, if it's inside. You could be the most beautiful woman in the world . . ."* and he remembered for her what Marilyn was supposed to be. Everywhere she went people wanted her to sign a paper or get her picture taken, and she had a lot of money and if ever there was anything she wanted, she could have it. And one night she just took a handful of pills and went to sleep and a lot of people couldn't understand why. He said, *"Roxie, it's all right to be dumb. Maybe it's best . . . some poor old cotton field man out there under the sun, he doesn't know anything but how to take two rows at a time and keep moving, doing a little singing to himself and maybe church on Sunday, not even able to read, just the kind of man that all those welfare folks feel they ought to do for, and if you told him what little he had to live for and offered him a handful of pills, he wouldn't even understand how you could talk that way."* And she scoffed at him. She said, "Toby, you'd make me believe that better if I saw you comin' out of a cotton field every day to a pot of beans and cornbread." And he laughed and said maybe she was right.

But Toby knew things she didn't know. More than one time she remembered how it was when she was on that farm and it didn't sound so good to her, but she wouldn't say anything to Toby about it because he'd just look at her and he'd know how sometimes she hurt inside, how she sobbed in the next room, and how she'd turn on him and tell him he could look like that all his life but she'd be goddamned if she'd admit that what she did made her feel guilty or that she was one goddamned bit sorry about anything, and she'd stand there defiantly and he'd look at her until she didn't want to stare into his eyes anymore and then he'd look away for her, making it easy, and take that pint from under his pillow and swallow once and put the cap back on carefully.

It was just that the world was so sad to Toby. He didn't see what other people saw maybe and he didn't fight it. He just did his thing and when they took him in for public drunk, it didn't really matter to him. He helped around the jailhouse and got to know all the police and listened to the stories they told about their kids and how, by God, this one was going to college . . . he was sure God going to see that his kid had a chance. Maybe that was it . . . there was some-

thing about Toby that told people they could confide . . .
they maybe *smelled* a kind of gentleness in him, knowing
somehow that he wasn't trying to get anything from them,
wasn't trying to use their bodies or cheat them with his mind
or steal from them . . . that he was just plain Toby, defense-
less, so why did anybody have to be afraid or feel threatened
by Toby? Like a child, as he was there on the bed now, hurt
and sick, and she wished, as she pressed close to him, as her
lips touched the long black fingers, she wished to God that
she could give him the kind of peace he needed.

The boys came back with the pills. They hovered over
the bed and the kid explained that one of those shots was to
put him out and that he wouldn't move a muscle for pretty
much a day. The pills were going to keep him doped until
his nerves got back in shape and in the meantime about
all he'd better have was soft stuff in his stomach, soup and
liquids, and within a week he'd be in decent shape.

The kid put the pills in the orange crate and asked Roxie
if she planned to sit with him for a while. She nodded,
though Levi suggested they might ought to go on now and
let him rest.

So she sat long into the night, hearing the sounds of the
trucks shifting down, a few blocks away at the stop sign.
Outside the window the summer bugs orbited the light that
no longer shined in his eyes, going no place, she thought,
just hungry to feel whatever it was about that light. And she
thought about the white man who ran the business up the
street who had phoned her saying he was coming tomorrow
and would pull his car up in the alley and take the back stairs
so he would not be seen. And then she'd do that for him again,
watch him get his eyes all crazy, twenty minutes after he'd
sold a new washing machine to some lady, he'd be up there
naked and dancing around like crazy while she threw
oranges at his body, pelting him, picking up two or three at

a time as they bounced off his body and pelting him some more until he was satisfied, and then he'd collapse and breathe hard for a time while she gathered up all the oranges and put them in a sack like he had brought them, and when he got dressed he'd thank her and take the sack of oranges and, by Jesus, she'd almost bet anything he'd go give them to somebody to eat.

Toby drew a deep breath and let out a kind of long moan and then he didn't breathe again for a time and she felt something terrible, afraid maybe he had died, until she clutched his arm and he drew in another breath. So she settled back in the wooden chair beside his bed and as she sat in that lonely darkness, unable to communicate with her man, like the moths flying suicidally into the light, something new occurred to her, something she had not known before about Toby . . . that long ago he had learned to expect and to accept the greater tragedy of man, that if a man took his wife away, he accepted his pain like a hound dog struck by an automobile and crawled for isolation under a shack and lay there licking his wounds, alone, until he survived or died . . . that if his country took his son in the prime of life and returned what was left of him to be placed in the red earth, he could retreat from this hideous misery and alone bear the suffering. And if he loved her, he could know that she lay with countless men in an adjoining room and of this pain he would not speak. And only when called upon, perhaps to save her life, as he had done with Sonny Hutto, would he intervene. And yet this last episode, this ghastly self-punishment had been triggered not because of man's capability to inflict great injury, which he had accepted time and again, but because of man's ability to be small and petty. The Assyrian—nearly at the cost of Toby's life and perhaps still, because the outcome was in doubt— had done no more than cheat him of a few dollars. Was it this pettiness that Toby could not tolerate? Was this his rage, his utter defiance of the cheap character of man? She remembered that once he told her he had been traveling from city to city and went into one of those roadside telephone booths to call a friend. He dialed the number correctly but a strange voice answered and informed him that his friend no longer lived there. So Toby dropped another dime into the slot and called Information. He reported that he was trying to reach his friend and that the number had been changed. Upon answering, the information operator returned his dime. Toby told her that he then asked the operator to connect him with his friend's new number but she explained that she could not do that, unless he dropped the dime back into the slot. He responded by saying that the telephone company was responsible for the publication of the directory and that he had made no error in dialing. Therefore, the ten cents he had invested was the responsibility of the telephone company and the operator should connect him with his party. The young lady repeated that she was unable to do this. He then asked her to release the original dime, give him the proper number, and he would dial his friend. This she told him was also impossible. He explained that when he called Information, she was able to return his dime and if she would simply punch whatever button again, he could have his original dime to place the call with.

She suggested that if he would write a letter explaining the situation, a dime would be sent to him. Toby became incensed and told her it would cost him five cents for a stamp to mail the letter of request, plus stationery and envelope. That, he said, would come to eight cents. The telephone company would send him a dime but he would still be eight cents the loser. The operator most curtly informed him that this was the only possibility. Toby insisted that if he must make this request by mail, the telephone company should send him ten cents plus five cents for the stamp plus three cents for the envelope and the stationery—a total of eighteen cents—which he would happily accept even though he had been deprived of the telephone visit with his friend.

The operator said this was totally unacceptable and the most he could expect, by whatever procedure, would be ten cents. At this time that thing which Roxanne had most recently discovered occurred, that thing that had initiated the obscene painting on the Assyrian's window.

Toby furiously began to kick out the glass in the telephone booth. Sounding like a duck being throttled, the operator began to scream near-unintelligible threats concerning prosecution for the destruction of telephone property. Toby took the receiver and began to bang it repeatedly against the telephone. The sound in the operator's ear must have been incredible. After kicking out all of the glass, he gave a tremendous yank on the wire connecting the receiver, suddenly drowning in silence the vehement protests of the operator. Knowing that a report of this violence would very shortly send the law, he quickly entered his automobile and left the scene.

As Toby reported it to Roxie one evening when reasonably intoxicated, he expressed a kind of quiet pleasure. And she thought that this was what had set off the recent experience from which he was now trying to survive. The man who lay before her, so serenely able to accept man's capacity for inflicting terrible pain upon his fellow man, had rebelled at the petty. This had been his weakness. She was not certain she was right about this because she had grown very weary sitting alone with him in the darkness, as his body suffered terrors which she could only imagine. She only knew that there was love, a feeling she received more than she gave,

and knew guiltily that was because of her own inadequacy,
never his. But the feeling was infectious. She gave to him as
she had never given to another man because he inspired the
freeness of it. Thus the hours passed, the long night leading
into the dull, sad morning, while he lay only breathing and
occasionally moaning from some dark misery about which
she did not know but could only wonder.

By the second day he was conscious, calmed by the pills
and the fluids, but in a kind of special misery. The next day
he was better and it was then that she took the boys with
her, to settle the charge.

The kid was silent most of the way, those two short blocks,
simply contributing his presence and not certain that it
would be to any avail. Levi drove them in the cab and he
mumbled about how the Assyrian would take all this. They
parked in front of the hot dog joint and went inside, seeing
the phallic sign had been removed. By chance, the Assyrian
was there this time, and not lying with his mistress. He eyed
them suspiciously, the fat bags under his eyes cynical.

They moved past the cash register, the four of them, the
kid, dressed in coat and tie, steaming in the heat of the
restaurant, Levi with his sport shirt sweat-stained from
the hours in the cab, Julius there to lend legal assistance, and
Roxie in a tight skirt and low-cut blouse. She went first,
leading them to the stools at the end of the counter, and
when the stringy-haired waitress came to take their orders,
Roxie told her they had business with the Assyrian. They
watched him wipe his hands on a chili-splattered apron.
When he paused in front of them, he leaned his big hands
on the counter, moving his eyes from one to the other until
he reached Roxie, and she saw the eyes change somewhat
and she knew the look.

"You got business with me?"

"It's about Toby . . . and the sign," she said.

The Assyrian nodded and pushed his lips out as if the name was distasteful to him. "So what about Toby?" he asked.

Julius cleared his throat and tried to explain. "Now there was the fact that you owed Toby a bill, had in fact for a long time. It was Toby's understanding that when he finished the sign, he would be paid. When the . . . lady . . . refused to pay him, he became angry and . . . well, he hasn't been well."

"Drunk," the Assyrian said.

"Now what it cost to remove the . . . offensive sign, we figure couldn't be more than the bill due him previously."

The Assyrian's eyes came back to Roxie, each time penetrating, not hostile but demanding, as though he knew he had them.

"It is true," Julius continued, "that a number of black people eat here. This is not a threat, of course . . ."

The Assyrian laughed at that, revealing teeth that had not been cleaned for perhaps a long while. He ran his hand through his hair and wiped it on his apron, and again his eyes came creeping back to her. "I got plenty business. I sell a good hot dog cheap. I never wanted for business. If your people don't want my dogs, that's for them to decide. This guy comes in here and makes a mess of my window and everybody laughs. I don't like that. So he broke the law. That's his problem."

"He's sick," Curtis said. "He ought not to be in jail."

And the dark eyes came back to her again. "So he won't get any cheap liquor in jail. It should be good for him."

Roxie leaned forward, resting her elbows on the counter, knowing the blouse fell open, watching as the Assyrian studied that exhibition. And she saw the lust there and said, "Maybe it wouldn't hurt to forget it . . . to not push it. Maybe you could find it in yourself to let it go . . ."

The eyes came up and seemed to dig holes in her and he clenched his teeth until the muscles of his jaws made small knots, and he kept looking at her. She understood perfectly and very slowly, with a small gesture, she nodded her head to him, hoping the others would not see, telling him *yes,* and seeing it in her face he took one hand from the counter and flipped it in the air, like tossing away a care, and flashed the dirty teeth.

"So . . . the guy made a mistake. All right. I got a big heart . . . you can tell him he's okay. I'll tell the cops it was all a mistake . . . it was a hot dog, only he wasn't a very good painter and some dirty-minded people got the wrong idea . . . so no charges. That make you feel better?"

She did not move, as the others, especially the kid, audibly breathed sighs of relief, letting Julius think maybe his argument had been effective . . . and Levi sliding off the stool, ready to get the hell out of there before the crazy bastard changed his mind, and as they began to move she remained briefly, seeing his eyes drift back to her, and the deal was made.

It came to her the next day when the cop on the block up the street passed the word that the Assyrian had said it was all a mistake and he didn't want any publicity and so forget the whole thing. And the cop told her he understood the solicitor didn't want to do anything with it anyway because it was so goddamned asinine. So it was done.

He came two days later. He walked up the stairs and rapped on her door and started taking off his shirt. "So we got your boy fixed up," he said.

Roxie got up from the bed and began to slip out of her robe. The Assyrian paused to watch that, studied the French bra—the one Toby had bought her—the bikini panties, white against the yellow skin, watched her dig a thumb into the elastic on either side and pull her arms down. She unsnapped the brassiere and let it fall free. When she reached the bed, he had that incipient grin on his fat face. She lay waiting for him, looking at the ceiling.

"I want a little French first," he said. "Then you can finish it straight."

She moved aside so that he could lie on his back and she performed that duty until he pushed her away. She turned over and he took her, big and heavy on her, hurting her breasts with his hands and making a sound in his throat that was like vengeful laughter. He would have gone on and on, but since he didn't deserve more, she performed a couple of tricks he hadn't expected and he lost control and collapsed, gasping for breath. With all her strength, Roxie rolled him away and, before he could get his breath, she was dressed again, drawing the robe about her body.

He studied her from the bed, ugly in his fat nakedness and knowing she had turned him out fast, faster than he wanted, but she had paid the price and there wasn't much he could say. She lighted a cigarette and started for the door.

"Pretty good girl," he said. "Maybe some other time."

"If you ever get a penis painted on your window . . . maybe, but I wouldn't count on it."

He laughed at her, but it was an empty laugh.

"Stay as long as you like," she said. "I'm leaving now."

She exhaled a tube of smoke, opened and closed the door behind her, and went down the hall to Levi's room. She turned on the television set, turned the volume high, and hoped Levi would not be back for a while. She curled up on his chair and closed her eyes tightly, feeling the tears seeping about the lids, and shuddered, fighting back the sob that rushed to her throat, feeling for the first time the way she had been told they all came to feel sooner or later. The only salvation was that none of them knew. They hadn't seen her silent negotiation and none of them had seen him come to her. And most important, perhaps, the only thing that saved her, was that Toby would never know. She turned off the set and listened for the heavy footsteps retreating along the hall. When she heard them, she returned to her room and slipped into a dress.

Toby was sleeping as she passed his door and she paused, only for a moment, to look into that quiet, calm face. Downstairs she sat at the bar and started hitting the beer like they were going to stop making it tomorrow and she didn't notice when Sonny Hutto came in and sat beside her and touched her arm.

"You ugly bastard," she said when she saw who it was, spitting the words through her teeth. "You sure God better keep your black ass away from me."

She had the bottle in her hand and in one motion she could have snapped it across the bar and in another she'd have his throat. She felt the hand release her and saw that glint of hate flicker across his face, but he moved away and in a few minutes was gone.

She put the empty bottle on the counter and ordered another. And after a while she stopped counting, just sat there looking straight into the flashing Budweiser sign until . . . maybe they went after him, but Levi came and put his arm around her waist and led her out of there and helped her upstairs where he gently made her lie down on her bed. The ceiling was turning around and she thought she might be sick, but gradually that passed.

"You all right now?" Levi asked.

She nodded.

"Toby's okay . . . he's better," he said.

"Yeah." She could hear the thick distorted sound in her voice. "Toby's okay now."

And that was all that mattered.

13

It was raining the first morning he eased down the stairs to the sign shop, a light mist that touched his face with a kiss-like coolness. Toby turned the corner at the bottom of the stairway and fumbled in his baggy trousers for the keys to the shop. The people on the street were seeing him for the first time in over a week—the last occasion had been his return, his feet dragging as they pulled him out of the cab, the kid taking most of the weight of his body as they began the climb. Now as the people passed, going to the pool hall or the little grocery or the bar or even up toward the railroad tracks leading to the main business section, they called to him and when he spoke, quite solemnly, they looked into his face to see what the last debauchery had done to him, and he thought probably noticed the thinness of his face, that less-than-energetic expression in his eyes. But he had made it, and most of the recollection was too dimmed, too out of focus to be a meaningful memory.

He located the key and opened the door to the shop, smelling the stale air, finding some mail stuck through the slot. He took it to his desk and began to sort through it. There was, it was suggested on one envelope, the possibility that he had won a hundred dollars for the rest of his life whether he subscribed to the magazine or not. He tossed the offer into the waste basket, thinking that a week ago, had he won, they might have got out cheaply and might still, depending on what he did with himself. And to this he had given a great deal of thought upstairs as his body began to respond to the medication and the food. He could not go on as he had. He did not want to go on that way and, though he had already experienced the dreams of some evil hand turning up that first drink of cheap whiskey, he knew that he lived with the choice of whether or not to take it, in despair or in joy. Lost in memory of a life past, he could make the decision, and if he made it wrong he was going to be back where he had been before and perhaps his troubled heart might not have the reserve for another time. He did not know what he would do, but as he sat at his desk he knew what he wanted to do.

He lifted a scrap of cardboard and took a charcoal pencil and began to sketch an S, the first one coming off badly, but he tried again and again until his hands worked with greater certainty.

Roxanne came in and sat in the chair behind his desk. "How do you feel?"

Toby turned and searched her face, so beautiful, young. "I'm fine," he said.

"Are you still taking the pills?"

"Yes."

Many times in the moments beyond delirium and through the growing occasions of clarity he had rehearsed the thoughts that came to his mind now.

"I don't want to go through that again," he said, placing the charcoal stick on his desk and turning to half-face her, so that he could escape her eyes if it became necessary.

"Jesus Christ, I sure hope to God you don't," she said.

He smiled. His voice was low, almost sad. "You said one time . . . a long time ago . . . I guess you said it several times . . ." He paused and collected the saliva in his mouth and swallowed. ". . . that you'd quit." He glanced and saw the change in her eyes, a curiosity there, an uncertainty about where this was leading.

"I told you I would," she said.

"I never wanted anybody to have to . . ." He looked down at his black hands and felt the small tremor remaining. ". . . to care. There was Toby and sometimes he was in jail and sometimes he was working good. If he was gone for a few days . . . well . . . and they just took me for what I was and I tried very hard not to hurt anybody, not anymore, and I think I found out that I didn't want anymore hurt either. I think I figured if they took me for what I was, that was fine, and if they didn't, then I could make it. I thought a lot about that when I was drinking, that everybody got along with Toby because he didn't mean anybody any harm. And it was that way, Roxie, for a long time, long before I met you. I just sipped along . . . until the whiskey got worse a little at a time, but I could still make it all right. Only now . . . what I'm telling you is I can't do that anymore."

"I know that," she said evenly.

"And I realized that I was wrong about some people . . . maybe more than I even knew. I put some people to a lot of trouble and they took care of me when it got bad. And I remembered all those times you made it easy for me to love you. Maybe I even made it hard for you to come to me because I never asked for you, never really asked for you to come to me. So I wondered about that, about you having always to give and how that must be to a woman. And I figured this last time, during this sickness, that there isn't any way to tell how much is left." He turned to her and saw the moisture at her eyes and he lowered his gaze to his hands, still seeing her beauty, and said softly, "I want you to quit, Roxie. I want you to move in with me. And if it really matters to you, like you told me once, if you want the baby, we could do that."

And then he was silent, tired and weary of this last sickness, knowing he was offering not very much perhaps, but offering, and very much terrified that it had changed, that all those times she had asked for him were over and that now she would not take him. He could not look from his hands. Then he heard her moving and caught his breath as she was there, going down by the chair and slipping her arms around his legs where he sat on the chair and covering his hands with her face in his lap, the softness of her hair falling across his fingers as she nodded against his legs . . . *Yes, Toby* . . . *yes.*

He took his hand free and stroked the face and saw the people passing by outside, some pausing for an instant, some only glancing and hurrying on, because whatever was transpiring in there, even in a store front on a public street in the middle of the morning, was a private thing.

In a while she got up and took his hand. He didn't even bother to lock the door of the shop but followed her, his arm around her waist, slowly up the stairs, feeling her head against his shoulder, and he said, "Sweetpot . . . if you ever leave me . . ."

"Oh, Toby."

"Don't tell me . . . just *go.*"

She did not answer. They reached his room and she closed the door as he sat in the wooden chair. At first she began to move about the room as though speculatively.

"There," she said, "on that wall. I want the painting . . . the doll."

"All right," he said.

"Then I want some lamps . . . something for evening, nice and pretty but not too bright, with a three-way bulb so we can turn it down for when you want to make love to me."

"Fine," he said.

"And the bed is okay . . . for now. I mean, it could be on the hardwood floor and it wouldn't matter, but someday, when you get back to painting signs and things are going pretty good . . ."

He looked at the bed. He understood. "Okay."

"And the goddamned orange crate nailed to the wall . . ."

He looked at it. It looked incredible there.

"Toby, we've seen some hard times together. Maybe we better leave that mother there to remind us."

He did not answer. He simply watched her in the process of making a tired old upstairs room into a home where one day she might bring her child. She was making a nest.

She stopped her pacing and kicked one shoe free, then the other. She lay on the bed next to the window and stretched her arms above her head, making the breasts rise. "Are you broke?" she asked.

"No. I rat-holed some along."

"You didn't drink it all?"

"No."

"I have some money," she said.

There was a strained silence. He did not want to talk about the money she made down the hall.

"Toby . . . maybe we could keep that for . . . you know, in case something happened."

He did not answer and when she looked to him from the bed he shrugged.

"Do you know," she said, "do you have any idea how much it means to me to not have to take that . . . that *mess* anymore?"

He did not reply.

"God, Toby . . . I'm home. I'm finally home."

He pushed the chair back and came to the bed. He stretched out beside her, felt her arm slip under his neck, and let his hand fall lightly, gently on her stomach. And he knew, from her feeling, that it was not a time for action. It was a time for peace. It had been a long time coming, this moment, and the other, the passion, the song of love would come later. But for now they lay together in peace, a man, a woman, pledged in simplicity and beauty to each other.

14

The autumn came, a kind of sneaky invasion, kissing a single dogwood leaf red, a warning to the green surrounding that the time was soon. From the mountains around Rutherfordton or perhaps from above, at Asheville, the cool drifted down to the Piedmont, giving the people a marvelously pleasant block of weather . . . clear, sunny skies but not searing with heat so the young women could lie beside the pools or on blankets in the grass more comfortably than before to absorb that color, and the men got out there on the country club golf course in great numbers, and the boats were thick on the lake, the water skiers following like contrails behind a high-flying jet . . . a beautiful time.

The black people sat on the porches long after dusk . . . a young man and woman strolling almost ghost-like in the growing darkness, soft outlines, and the kids who long before had worn down the grass on the vacant lot strained their eyes against the coming darkness for just one more inning, one more time at bat . . . *throw it, baby . . . I gonna knock this one home to Willie Mays' house.* And the lovers paused at the corner, bathed in the soft glow from the light pole, and she leaned against the wood, her head thrown back to the sky to see the first of stars as he moved his hands to her waist and felt her thighs against him . . . *Baby, we gonna have us some love* . . . and he nuzzled his lips against her neck until she squirmed, that pelvis moving ever so slightly . . . *you gonna get hell beat out of you is what* . . . and he laughed and said again, "Baby, we gonna get us some love . . ." and she whirled away suddenly but took his hand as her skirt flared out for an instant, laughing, her teeth white in the light, and let him lead her on down the street as the air cooled.

The lawn mowers were being oiled and put away and the black men who worked the yards got out the leaf rakes, those black hands gripping the handles like they were made to fit . . . it wouldn't be long. And the J. C. Penney store alarmed the young, too soon, too eager, it seemed, with the Back to School advertisements.

On the block, little changed except that in the evenings the young studs came to the bar wearing long-sleeved turtle-necks and the women sometimes carried sweaters. The men sat in the booths looking at the long-legged women with those short skirts, imagining. The guys with the nice pads not so worried once they could get that dark gal there, but the others, the poor studs who had to depend on the back seats of automobiles . . . those short skirts were nice, but *be damned* those panty hose, like a chastity belt almost . . . but then, there were always problems.

And in the pool hall the hustlers stood about waiting, cigarettes dangling from their mouths, keenly watching a game, watching how good that buck could make that cue slide like it was bathed in oil through his fingers . . . *you watch that cat . . . he come in from out of town and he don't shoot too good 'til you get the long green down there and*

*then his eyes come into focus and you can tell the way he
lines up that shot he knows just where that cue ball is going
to stop on that table for the next shot . . . just so sweet to
make the next one easy, and the one after that . . . and baby,
you done lost your wad before you got a chance to hitch up
your pants for a shot . . . yeah, he playin' bad now, but when
the money's on the line, look out, baby.*

And the cop stands on the corner near the tracks and
twirls that billy, lazy-like, but his eyes miss very little down
the block. There is a freshly painted stack of cardboard
signs, finished and dried and ready for delivery in the morning. The word has spread. Toby is back in business, not just
back in business but out there on the street hustling.

The money came in and when he became tired, there was
the thought of that thirst and then the thought of that sickness, and he passed the taproom and climbed the stairs where
she was fixing something, where she opened that small refrigerator she had bought and gave him a glass of cold grapefruit juice so he could have a drink and not think about the
other, and where she put a skillet on the hot plate she got at
the pawnshop. And in a few minutes, as he lay back on the
bed, stretched out and loose, he smelled the meat in the pan
and it did not seem like six weeks had passed.

He lay watching her back as she worked. She wore some
kind of jersey blouse, something that looked glued to her
body, and he could see the concave line down her spine.

"You do pretty good today?" she asked, flipping a piece of
meat to the other side in the skillet.

"Pretty good," he said and sipped the grapefruit juice.

"Makin' me some money to spend?"

He chuckled.

" 'Cause I bought us a present today."

He looked up with that, from the rim of the glass to her
shoulders, and he waited until she turned. Things had been

good and he'd been bringing it in, giving the cash to her,
letting her take the checks to the bank, and just slightly terrified that she might announce they had made a down payment on a goddam Cadillac.

She opened the dresser drawer and came out with it, all
wrapped in some fancy paper, and carried it to where he
lay on the bed, sitting beside him. "Okay. Tear off the paper."

"No . . . you."

She ripped away the wrapping, enough that he could see
the radio. Battery operated, AM and FM. She turned it on
and found some music.

"Good tone," he said.

"Sometimes . . . when you have trouble sleeping, I figured
you could turn it down low and listen."

"How much?"

"Not much."

"Is it new?"

She grinned. "Well . . . almost." She put it on the floor and
leaned against him. "Was that all right?"

"Yes . . . that was fine."

She ran her hands to his face and traced the line of his jaw
with her finger.

"How are we on money?" he asked.

"Fine."

"What does that mean?"

"That means that if you keep on like you have, we may
take us a trip to the beach for a few days."

"I'm afraid of that ocean," he said lightly. "I liked to got
myself killed there once."

"You about drowned?"

"No . . . this lady had this cabin. Hell, she didn't tell me
anything about a man . . . she was just going down the beach
and I said, 'Hey, baby,' and she came over and plopped down
and we got to talking and I gave her a drink of my liquor

and pretty soon she just invited me to come over to her place for a visit. So one thing led to another and I got all relaxed and then I heard this car door slam and she was up like a shot and told me to haul my ass out the back door.

"It was good dark then so I grabbed everything I could get my hands on . . . I got my pants and shirt but I dropped my shoes. All the time she's about to blow her mind, and so I jerked open that little back door and ran out . . . only I didn't run; I flat flew because some dumb jackass had built a back door to the cabin but he never got around to building the steps, and I fell four and a half feet and nearly broke my leg.

"I heard him making a racket and I knew I couldn't run on that leg, so I grabbed my stuff . . . the cabin was kind of on stilts . . . and I rolled back under the house about the time he jerked open the door, giving her all kinds of hell, like how he was going to kill me right now . . . Now, that's a thing I never understood . . . why the man always wants to kill the other man. He's got to figure that as long as the man hasn't beat hell out of her, she *had* to invite him in for a good time, but they always want to kill the man. Well . . . he's been around that cabin, so he knew better than to step off that four and a half feet, and she kept saying, 'Honey, baby . . . they ain't been nobody here,' and he picked up that shoe of mine and slammed it down on the floor over my head and said he was going to get a knife and cut my balls off and stick one in each ear.

"Pretty soon he came around the house—I guess he was drunk and I'd bet a dollar he'd been lying with some woman himself—but he didn't have a flashlight and he couldn't see anything, and all the time I am lying very still, holding my knee, knowing I couldn't run ten feet before he cut me, and after a while he went back inside and got to beating the hell out of her, making a racket, so I crawled out from under

there and hobbled away. But, sweetpot, I got to tell you that
first step was a lulu."

She was smiling. "You deserved to break your leg," she
said. "How many women you had, Toby?" she asked thoughtfully.

He looked at her curiously. "That's no question to ask."

"How many? I bet you been on more beds than Spring-
maid sheets."

He laughed.

"How many?" she asked again, and he thought briefly of
her working in the room next door and thought he could tell
her they were probably about even, or maybe she had a lead
on him . . . but knew it was cruel to even think about that
anymore.

"Three," he said.

"Shit."

"My wife, that lady in the cabin, and you."

He watched her throw back her head to laugh, saw the
lovely line of her neck, and reached over to brush her breast
with his hand. She slid away from him and went to the hot
plate where she took the meat from the skillet and put it on
the plates, and in a few minutes she set up the TV tables.
He sat on the bed and she pulled up the chair and they ate.

"One time I had a car," he said. "I never could drive
very well, even sober, but one night near sundown I found
out I was about out of liquor and I only had a few minutes,
so I jumped in the damned thing and took off lickety-split to
get there before the liquor store closed and there was this
hill that went down the parking lot to the store and I hit the
brakes, but there weren't any brakes . . . just gone, and there
wasn't anyplace to go, baby. It was right through that liquor
store window. Lucky thing it had already closed, but that car
plowed through the glass, hit the counter, tore that down . . .
then I rolled through the gin section, on past the vodka,

through the scotch, and came to a stop right in front of the bourbon. You never smelled anything like it in your life. So I just rolled down the window of the car and reached out and took a bottle of bourbon, broke the seal on it, and sat there waiting until they got there . . . the police . . . and when they came in I told them my brakes failed. They asked if I was drinking, so I did the decent thing . . . I offered them a drink. Since I figured I had just bought me a whole big goddamned bunch of liquor anyway, I said I figured I might as well have a drink.

"Well, they'd have really put me way back in the jailhouse on that one, but they investigated the car and found that something had happened to the hydraulic line and I *had* lost my brakes, like I said, so my insurance man had hysterics. They *could* prove I was maybe crazy, sitting there drinking some of that man's liquor, but they *couldn't* prove that I had had a drink before I got there. I guess I'll remember all my life that policeman stepping through all that broken glass and looking in the window of my car, and I said just as polite as could be, 'Good evening, Officer.' Anyway, that was the last car I ever owned. Funny thing, a couple of years later the insurance man built a new building and I painted all the signs for his place. He wasn't a bad fellow." He put down his fork. "That was good, Roxanne . . . real good."

She began to clean away the dishes and he heard Levi's heavy feet on the stairs. He came in carrying his sack which Toby knew to contain beer.

"Come in, Levi."

"I better go on down . . . there's a TV show on in a few minutes."

"Levi, you can drink that beer, you can spill it on the floor, you can take a goddamned bath in it and it won't make any difference. If you don't stop trying to hide from us, we'll get offended."

Levi came on in, reluctantly almost, glancing at Roxie to determine whether Toby was telling it like it was or if he'd lose his head and grab a can and gulp it down. Roxie pointed to a chair. She took the beer and put it into the refrigerator and snapped open a can for Levi.

"I was just telling Roxanne how much trouble I've had in my life with glass."

"Glass?" Levi asked. He took a sip of the beer and wiped his brow with his sleeve.

"Yeah . . . one time I was up in Charlotte with another chap—Divinity Aycock—and we were in this beer place and we'd had about a bellyful. Next door they were putting up brick and fixing this nice big window they were about to put in. The plate glass was on one of those trucks, leaning at an angle and all tied down, like you've seen, and this guy, Divinity, got to telling me how all his life he had wanted to throw a brick through a pane of glass like that. Well, he got to talking about it and had another beer or two and it seemed he was just plain obsessed."

"Just what?"

"Just couldn't get it out of his mind. Like he said, if he thought he died before he did that, he'd never forgive himself. So we got to figuring about it and neither one of us had any money to speak of, and I told him the glass probably cost less than a hundred dollars and they'd probably only give him thirty days for doing it anyway, so why didn't he just pick up one of those bricks when we left and haul back and throw it through the glass and get it over with? And he told me how good it would sound, the crash and then the pieces hitting the street and sliding along. I told him he was just about honor bound to throw that brick when we left.

Well, he got me kind of interested, because I understood how much he wanted to do it. So suddenly he put his beer bottle down and got up, like a man in a trance. I followed him outside . . . telling him to run like hell after he did it and probably he wouldn't even get caught. He went out of that bar and stood there for a minute and I figured he was about to pick up one of those bricks and get it done, but little by little his shoulders began to sag and he started off down the street. Well, I caught him by the arm and I told him he would worry about it the rest of his life if he didn't go back there and throw that goddamned brick . . . but his eyes got kind of sad and he just shook his head. I yelled at him, 'You got to! Don't you understand?' But he just turned away.

"So I went back and took one of those bricks and sailed that mother twenty feet, square through that plate glass . . . and you know he was right? It makes a hell of a sound. Well, he ran like mad and I stood there so pleased about the whole thing that these two guys from the glass company came over and got me by the arms and pushed me down and sat on me. And the police came and asked me how come I did that. I said I did it for my friend. They said what friend? He was long gone by then. So they took me down and booked me. It made so little sense that they brought in a psychiatrist to talk to me. He talked a long time about it and before it was over he was shaking his head like he understood that maybe everybody wanted to do that at least once in his life and he was sorry he couldn't have been there to see it. How do you like our new radio?" He leaned from the bed to turn up the volume.

Levi listened for a time and approved but kept looking at his watch, and Toby knew he wanted to get down to his room to see some spy go out on a mission, so he gestured to Roxie.

"Give Levi his beer. He's missing his show."

In a moment Levi was down the hall. Roxie came and sat beside him in the chair.

"I got caught up today," Toby said. "I had about three, four hours and I painted a little."

"You did?"

"Yeah . . . the face of a woman. Arrogant but sensitive too. Beautiful woman . . ."

"What woman?" she asked, her voice nearing an edge.

"Good lookin' young woman, with dark eyes, and in the painting she's looking right at you with her lips slightly parted, like she loves you, like she wants your baby . . . but cool. Nice and easy. And when you look at the picture you just know that when you get to bed with that woman she'll love you like God wouldn't believe possible."

Her lips were beginning to tighten.

"It's down there . . . I've got another day or two to polish it up, but I got what I wanted today. The rest is finishing work."

She did not say a word. Her movements were jerky and she took the keys from the fruit box and went out the door, shaking the old building when it slammed behind her, and he lay listening to her heels stepping rapidly down the stairs. He took a cigarette from his pocket and lighted it and watched it burn until it was mostly gone before he heard her coming back, slowly now, down the hall and she pushed open the door, standing there with the keys dangling in one hand and her lip trembling. She closed the door and came to him and pressed her body close.

"Toby . . . it's beautiful. You never said . . ."

"I know."

"Is that the way I look at you . . . those times?"

"Yes."

He leaned over her body and touched the volume on the radio, turning it slightly higher. Then he reached above his head and turned the lamp switch twice until only a soft glow remained.

15

Sonny Hutto lay on the bare mattress in his sister's house, alone now. She had gone early in the morning to maid for that white family. At noon he had considered a sandwich but when he opened the refrigerator and saw nothing appetizing, he took a can of beer instead, hesitated, took another, and made his way back to the small bedroom. He opened the first can and took one of the black beauties in one swallow, and in a few minutes that nice sensation came to his head. He turned on the radio and drew the shade to keep out some of the afternoon light. In a while he took another pill and finished the beer. It was pretty good, all right, with seven hundred dollars in his wallet, nice and easy. He remembered that time the head doctor at the prison left the room to answer a call, and he had looked at his records. He thought about the number—80. They measured his brain somehow and found out he had an eighty, which was pretty good, though he didn't let on that he knew, when the doctor came back in. He conned that man, dumbass white man with his books and his black spectacles, wanting to know all about how it was when he was a kid . . . so

he made it big and watched the doctor write it all down . . .
yeah, daddy . . . Sonny had to make it on his own . . . the old
man workin' for the county when he wasn't drunked up . . .
and the girls always got what there was first . . . that bed
. . . the year they had the twins and they told Sonny he had
to sleep on the floor by the stove and gave him them blankets
and the hard floor . . . shit! They thought he didn't know . . .
and they got them pretty print dresses when they went to
school and he wore those shoes they got down to the Salvation Army in the winter or the tennis shoes without socks,
and in the summer just bare feet. Shit, he knew what was
going on. As he lay on the bed he reached over to the small
table and took the revolver and fondled it, studying the
smooth polish of the blue metal. All that shit they did in
school . . . no matter what, because he was big he'd get it,
that strap. Goddam, he had a lot of that strap, but he never
cried . . . they could bust his ass until he was bloody and he
never let out a sound.

Then came the time in the fifth grade, though the other
kids had gone on ahead, they punished him because he was
tougher than the others and they made him stay in grade five
. . . and that old man got to swinging that strap and all of a
sudden he knew, and he turned around and jerked that strap
out of his hands and slapped the old man across the face. He
could still remember the look in his eyes when Sonny went
after him, the little old man running down the hall, and that
was the end of putting up with those people.

So his old man put him in the field with a truckload of
niggers to chop that cotton and he could chop that cotton
better than any of them . . . gain a whole row every two
rows, except the goddam boss man said he cut too many cotton plants, but what the shit, the boll weevil would have got
it anyway. He got big and strong, and after that they didn't
say much to Sonny unless they wanted a broke head . . . and

then it was easy. Didn't have to stand out in that sun all day.
He got him a jack and could strip the two rear wheels off a
car in no time at all and the white man at the junkyard gave
him four dollars apiece and never asked a goddam question,
until that squad car come around the corner that night, and
when he ran, nearly making it in the darkness, they got him
with that slug in the leg. So, man, it was a war, and when
they let him out of jail, he decided to use all that big 80 in his
head and go for the places in Yorksboro. He went in just as
calm as could be and held that pistol at that little grocery
store, and man, she couldn't move fast enough to put that
money in the sack . . . but that was before he got sent up the
last time, because you couldn't pull it off in Yorksboro . . . not
like now. When he got out again, he got that car and drove
to Charlotte at night, because Charlotte was big and those
late-hour grocery stores usually had some good money waiting. He got him a lady's stocking and pulled it over his face
just before he went in. There had been seven robberies already and they had picked up every dumb bastard they
could think of in Charlotte, but they didn't have that big 80
going for them, because all the time he was sitting down
there in Yorksboro laughing at them. The way it was going,
they'd never find him.

One day they had a drawing in the newspaper. It didn't
look much like him, except that he was big and maybe some
pig would figure something out, and so he thought it was
about time to go on someplace else. He didn't need his sister's place anymore . . . not with that big roll. He could go
down to Columbia or maybe to Washington and have himself a good time and get some more of those late-night grocery stores and some filling stations.

He took another of the black pills and felt like he was going to float right off that mattress. So he'd wait until dark and
go tonight, because there was just one more thing to do and

he couldn't leave until he got that done. Nobody got to Sonny
. . . that had to be. He remembered that smart-ass in the
prison, the time he threw a tray of food in his face. He took
a long look at that man and knew that someday he was
going to get his chance. And he did. They were working on
the garbage truck and Sonny waited until the load was in
and the door was starting to crush it, and he hit this man on
the back of the neck and just bent him half over into the
closing door and watched that mother turn into two pieces of
meat. And then he yelled that the driver should stop the
door because the man was being hurt. Nobody ever said a
word . . . they just asked him what happened and he said the
man slipped and fell into the opening and he didn't notice
until it was too late. Yeah, baby.

Sonny grinned and took another sip of the beer. Nobody
fingered Sonny Hutto. You touch Sonny and you got to pay.
He couldn't get that skinny bastard out of his mind . . . and
before he left for good, when it got dark, he'd pull that car
up outside and leave the motor idling and slip up the stairs,
and in a few minutes he'd come down and drive to Washington, just a nice drive in the night to Washington, and by
morning he'd take that seven hundred dollars and have himself a party. He fondled the pistol, opened the chamber and
let the slugs fall into his large hand . . . hollow points that
went in small and came out like a cannonball. Old Kennedy
found that out. He knew that kid was smart because he used
hollow points and when that lead got through opening up, he
had fifty pieces of it floating in his brain instead of a solid
slug that might have glanced off or got stuck in the bone.

He sipped the beer and remembered that ball bat and the
little fucker that looked like Mickey Mantle ready to send
one out of the park, so he had to use that big 80 and let the
little man have his day because he knew he'd have swung
that bat, sure as God. He had sat there in that room and lis-

tened to the man, nice and easy, and nearly laughed when the little man tossed him the pistol, empty, like he didn't figure Sonny could find another box of shells for a dollar and a quarter.

Sonny replaced the shells carefully. The pills had kissed his brain to a sweet glow. He would lie there and think about it for a while, a couple of hours, until it was dark, and then he'd go see the little man and take a nice trip to Washington.

The air was cool when he left the room. He had taken two more of the black beauties and he felt like he was walking on air. He slipped into his jacket and slid the pistol into his belt. His sister was back, sitting in that shabby room in the front, looking at the television while her old man was out working a second job, breaking his goddam back to keep it all going.

Sonny reached the door. "I'll be back."

She only glanced up and nodded. Outside he let the screen door close quietly and almost laughed to himself. He didn't say when, did he? He started the Ford and checked the gas gauge. Wouldn't be no use stopping, once he left the corner. He drove to the Texaco station and had the tank filled, made the dumb white bastard check the oil and the transmission and put air in the tires, and he was just waiting to see if the bastard was going to wipe his windshield, but he did, and Sonny took out the billfold and gave him the money.

He scratched out of the station, just to piss the attendant, then slowed it down because a man with an 80 brain didn't drive crazy with a nice fat pistol in his belt and a little payment due the skinny guy upstairs.

He found a parking place and eased into it, cutting his lights and looking around. Nothing much on Tuesday . . . nice and quiet. Only a few spades on the street. He had opened the door to the car, the Ford motor still purring sweetly, when he saw the woman come down the stairs. She turned and went down the street, crossing at the corner, go-

ing toward the cab stand. She walked up to a cab parked
there and stood talking to somebody. Sonny slipped out of
the car quickly and let the door metal touch but not close.
He took the stairs on quiet feet. When he got to the top, he
was breathing hard so he paused a moment, looking down the
hallway, seeing only the dull glow of the bulb at the far end.
He heard music coming from the second room . . . that was
the one. He eased down the hallway, making no sound, the
feel of the pistol nice and heavy in his hand. The door to
the room was open three or four inches and a slice of light
fanned out into the hall. He reached the door and shoved it
open suddenly and there he was, cute little bastard without
his baseball bat now . . . just lying there on the bed with
a magazine in his hand. He turned and Sonny grinned.

"Hiya, baby . . . I been missin' you."

The man's tongue came out like a snake and it traveled
around the lips and he squinted from behind those gold-
rimmed glasses, raising up slowly to his elbows. "Sonny, use
your head," he said.

And he thought of his 80 and the car idling downstairs
and the nice ride to Washington and the seven hundred dollars . . . and that dirty little fucker holding that baseball bat
on him when he was in the room with the girl.

"Hey, Mantle . . . where's your bat?"

The man shook his head, coming up some more on the bed.
Sonny thought maybe he was going to make a move . . . he
might have a gun someplace, and it was time to go because
he had had the pleasure of seeing what he was seeing in that
face. He snapped the trigger and the man jumped in a spasm
and tried to crawl from the bed. He snapped the hammer
again and his body jerked toward the wall and he was pushing the bed away from the wall. He snapped the trigger
again and saw the blood fly and spatter the window before

the body slipped behind and under the bed, and that was it
. . . he had him good.

Sonny moved rapidly down the hallway and saw a door
open at the far end and he turned as he reached the stairs
and sent a shot down the hall toward the man in the door
. . . it looked like a white boy and he made a dive back into
the room, and then Sonny was taking the steps two or three
at a time. He swept out as he heard a scream from someplace and started toward the Ford, had reached the fender
when the cop came running, and he knew that by the time
he got behind the wheel the cop would be too close, so he
squatted and leveled the pistol on his free arm and squeezed
off the shot and the cop rolled as he hit the sidewalk. Then
Sonny was up and around the car, ready to jerk open the
door when the cop, on his knees, began to unload that thirty-
eight.

But he figured he had that beat and everybody else was
running for someplace to hide. He swung the door open and
the shot came through the window and caught him on the
side of the neck and then the cop fell forward. He whipped
the wheels and cut out of the parking place, scratching out
of there, running a red light at the intersection, laughing to
himself, moving straight toward the highway and easing up
on the gas because he didn't want to pick up a squad car.

From there it was strictly cool, man, all of those 80 working
with those black beauties . . . down the main drag for a mile
to the turnoff, nearly ready for the bypass and out of town
when the dizziness started in his head and he could feel the
wet on his shirt front. He touched the wound and felt the
raw muscle in his neck . . . started to make the turn at the
gas station when the blindness came and he jerked the wheel,
afraid of cutting too wide with the Ford, and then the car
seemed to weave and suddenly hit something hard, so hard
it jerked him forward into the windshield and for an instant

he could see and tried to think what he was going to do now that he'd hit something, and then the flames came up in front of the car, a huge ball of flame, and he thought it must have been the gas pump. He was going to shift into reverse and maybe cut out of there when a new wave of dizziness came over him and he was going blind. And suddenly there was nothing, nothing at all except the feeling of being lifted, car and all, and the brilliant glow of fire.

Where there had been few people, suddenly they seemed everywhere. They were gathered about the body of the police officer who lay face down where he had fallen. The bullet had hit him in the chest on the right side, and a bright patch of blood had soaked his back. One knee was curled under his body, as though when he fell he was trying to regain his balance. His service revolver was still in his hand.

And in those moments after the first muffled, distant sounds had died away, Roxie glanced from Levi who sat in the cab. She looked around and saw nothing but she knew that someone, maybe down in the bar, had gone after somebody. Levi told her to get in the cab because all hell was about to break loose . . . already the cop was coming from up the street by the railroad tracks, reaching for his revolver. And then she saw the man dart out of the stairwell and in that instant recognized the face and she knew . . . God . . . God, Levi . . . and she was getting out of the cab when he reached over the seat and grabbed her arm as the shots recurred, the man shooting, the officer falling, only to rise and return the fire, and then the man was in his car and gone . . . whipping around the corner.

She made it across the street as cars began to stop, ran up the stairs before Levi, and threw open the door. She saw nothing and breathed *Thank God* an instant before she saw the blood on the window and noticed the bed pushed away.

"Levi . . . get an ambulance. Levi, hurry."

She pulled the bed away from the wall and, because he was still partly supported by it, he rolled toward her. He arched his back, his mouth sprung open as he drew in air. Then Curtis was behind her, pulling her away, telling her he had to see how bad it was.

Toby coughed and a fine spray of blood issued forth as she knelt beside Curtis. His eyes turned to her and he moved his hand out for her. She felt the fingers close about her arm.

"Oh, God, Toby."

She felt the pressure of his hand and then the blood as it came from the wound and saw where the bullet had taken part of the muscle of his arm. The kid had opened his shirt and she could see where the bullet had entered his lower chest. There was more blood just below his belt and she could remember hearing those three sounds, almost like a dog barking, in the distance. He was trying to move because he could not breathe.

"Help me turn him on his side," Curtis said, and Toby released his grip on her arm as they turned him. In the distance, as though from far away, they heard the cry of the ambulance, and no sooner had she heard the sound, praying for it to speed, than Levi was back up the stairs and coming into the room. He moved around behind her, tried to lift her away, but she resisted, feeling the pressure of Levi's arms against her shoulders. *Please.* And they waited, not speaking, listening to the siren approach so very, very slowly.

He did not want her to leave. He turned his eyes and saw the blood on her dress but he could not touch her because they had him turned on his side. It was easier now . . . he could breathe. The pain was not as bad as it had been. And he thought that it was too much to believe . . . a ruined liver and a damaged heart, and some insane fool had to come in with a pistol and hit him. As he waited he wondered how bad it was or, if it was bad, how lucky he was going to be when they got to him. Because this wasn't going to get him. He'd known for a long, long time how it was coming. It would come to his chest as he sat downstairs painting and he would simply lean forward against the easel and it would be over. But not this way. He had never been so sure of anything in his life, and he wished he could tell Roxanne not to worry.

They came into the room, breathless, the stretcher left outside the door. "Back, please," one of them said.

Roxie moved away. Levi and Curtis stood just outside the door as they lifted him and placed him on the stretcher. Levi said, "The cab . . . come on . . . the cab."

But she wasn't going with the cab. She was going with Toby.

"Easy," one of them said. The stairway was steep and they were breathing hard as they tried to keep the stretcher level. At the bottom, when they loaded him into the ambulance, she heard the woman shriek, "Oh, Jesus . . . it's Toby. Toby . . ."

They let Roxie inside as the driver slammed the door and got behind the wheel, and she saw them take the mask and put it over his mouth, and the man said, "Just slow and easy . . . you'll be all right."

It was like a moving picture, the film speeded too fast, when they reached the emergency entrance. They had him out of there and the doctor was already waiting. She followed, seeing them stare at the blood on her dress, and heard somebody say, ". . . a nigger shooting . . ."

She stayed with the stretcher . . . into the X-ray room, knowing that they had to find out what those bullets had done inside of him. It took only a very short time, and they wheeled him out into the hall and she stepped in front of the cart. The white attendant wanted her to get out of the way but hesitated just long enough for her to bend over him and look into his face. He was trying to say something to her, his tongue coming to his lips, as they opened and closed, and the doctor swept by suddenly.

"All right . . . into surgery. Let's go."

As she started to follow, a nurse, a large woman, restrained her and led her to a couch in the emergency room where she sat, knowing that all she could do now was wait, and looked across at a little boy who sat with a cast on his arm, his small face shocked by what he saw, and in a moment his mother took him out of the room. As soon as they had gone, she felt Levi's arm around her, drawing her against him, and Curtis sat across where the little boy had been.

Levi said, "We heard it wasn't too bad."

"He'll be all right," the kid said, and his voice trembled.

They had given him a shot and as he stared into the lights above, he knew they were prepared to operate. The doctor was giving curt orders. He asked, "How does it look?" but could not hear the sound of his voice and was not certain that he had said it at all. But he didn't think he was going to lose. Not this time. He was going to make it. He only wished they would tell Roxanne because she was coming apart.

He heard the doctor say, "All right . . . let's go."

They were gathered around her when the doctor came to the waiting room. She looked into his face. He was smoking a cigarette but still had that white cap on his head. "Are you his wife?" he asked.

"Yes."

"Bring her with me," he said to Levi.

She felt Levi's arm about her. Yeah . . . Toby made it.

Oh, God . . . in trouble, hurt bad, but he was going to tell
her how he was coming along now . . .

The doctor opened a door to a small office and went behind a desk. She sat across from him while Levi and the kid
stood behind. The doctor took a last puff on his cigarette
and looked at Levi first, then at Curtis. He stubbed out the
cigarette. "He died on the table," he said. "We didn't even
have time to try to repair. There was no hope." He looked
down and opened a drawer in the desk.

Levi's hand fell on her shoulder and she did not make a
sound but she could hear Levi sobbing behind her.

The doctor took two tablets from a cellophane wrapper
and reached for a pitcher of water from which he filled a
glass. "Take these," he said.

She took the tablets from his hand and he held the glass
of water until she accepted it and took the tablets.

The doctor turned to the kid. "Will you see, for her, that
the proper information is registered at the desk?"

"Yes, sir."

The doctor stood. "I'm very sorry," he said and went to the
door. "Stay here as long as you like. It's private." He closed
the door behind him.

Curtis said, "I'll go tell them what they need to know."

She lifted her head then. "Tell them . . ." Her voice broke.
"Listen to me . . ." She could not go on. "Please . . ."

They waited.

"I was his *wife*," she said softly.

The kid closed the door and was gone. She heard Levi
weeping and she stood and breathed a deep sigh.

"Levi."

He nodded, standing there like a great bear, his face
stained with tears.

"Take me home now."

He turned to the door.

The cab traveled slowly. A group of teenagers swept by in a car, their gay laughter filling the night. Off the road a huge screen of the outdoor theater was filled with color, a man and a woman dining at a luxurious table. The cab stopped for a red light. Two couples walked hand in hand, leisurely, across the street. She watched them, a young boy, laughing self-consciously, and her eyes caught those young black fingers intertwined. She did not weep until she saw that.

16

He was a young man and when she sat in his study and crossed her legs, it was apparent that he observed and approved. She had heard about him.

As far as she was concerned, one preacher was no better than another, but it was very important to her, now that he was gone, that it should be right, and if the young preacher intended to turn it into a civil rights speech, then he'd better get his ass ready for a walkout of her own.

"I came to tell you about Toby," she said.

He nodded respectfully. He wore a thin dark moustache and his hair was done in a modified Afro, which she didn't trust very much. His eyes were keen, very alert. He took a pad and a ball-point pen. "Yes, Mrs. Snow . . . I'd like to know. He didn't attend services, so I never had the privilege of knowing him."

Roxie blinked slowly. "All right, let me put it to you straight. No son of a bitch is going to ruin this. It's going to be right . . . like it was."

The preacher's eyebrows lifted slightly at her remark. "Go ahead, Mrs. Snow," he said.

"Toby was a man. He was a black man, but Toby never seemed to realize that. He did his thing and he got along with everybody . . . at least most of the time. So don't give us any of that long-suffering crap."

The preacher nodded, making notes, his eye catching her thigh quickly.

"He drank too much," she said. "Everybody who will be out there has seen him drunk . . . well, not like falling down, though he did that too, but mostly just about half-pickled and his mind was best then, sometimes. So you ought to mention that Toby hit the bottle. And he walked the streets at night. He'd look at the trees and the buildings . . . stop and look in the windows, like a kid, and talk to anybody who wanted to talk, and a lot of them did. There was a sadness about Toby and only a few people knew why, but that wasn't what made him drink. He drank that way before those things happened. And if it got worse, it was going to get worse anyway. He was a gentle and tolerant man, except when somebody did a small or petty thing and then he could be mean as hell, but mostly people were good to Toby because they sensed a kind of gentle soul. He wasn't after anybody . . . didn't want to take anything away from anybody. I can't remember him ever trying to make anybody feel bad just to make himself feel big. He listened to the goddamdest bunch of garbage you ever heard of from every kind of nut that walked the streets, including me, and when we got through piling all that crap on him, he went away maybe feeling sad for us, but we knew that somebody understood . . . or at least would give us the time of day and listen. How many people you know like that, preacher?"

The eyes came up from the notebook. "Not enough, I'm afraid."

"So say he was gentle and tolerant and kind and that he drank too much bad whiskey until the last several months of his life, and then he quit and he was making it too, because I knew. He did it for himself, and in a little way he did it for me and a few other people but mostly because he found out he couldn't handle it anymore, so he just quit."

"We don't usually mention a man's faults," the preacher said.

"Well . . . do it this time, only tell them that after all those years he made it."

The preacher nodded, though he seemed skeptical.

"Now, you'll have at least five policemen sitting out there. One is black and the others are white. One is the jailer. They all loved Toby. They'd pick him up drunk . . . never creating a disturbance. He never did anything really violent that I know of except save my life one time and paint a goddam sign on a man's window. Oh, he broke up a telephone booth and threw a brick through a plate glass window . . ."

The preacher lowered the note pad, thinking perhaps that this was not exactly an exemplification of a mild man.

"But all that stuff was either to help somebody or to get even with some real first class bastard or sometimes it was just some drunk stunt. Anyway when he was in jail—and they usually put him in there to keep him from stepping in front of a milk truck or something—he got to know those policemen, got to know all about their families. While those other clowns were sitting on their asses, he was cleaning the place up without being asked and when the Chief got appointed and he was in jail for being drunk, he went out there and painted his name on the office door . . . so you say that while Toby was in jail a lot, those who are hearing you talk, who knew him, figured he was like a guest. Toby was in jail to be protected against himself . . . not anybody else. Now you make that clear."

"Yes."

"Then there were the women . . . there will be a lot of

women out there who have slept with Toby, especially from a time before two years ago, back down the years. They'll want to know that Toby touched their bodies like nothing mattered, except that when it was over they felt something good and quiet inside. When Toby made love, he wasn't proving anything to himself . . . he didn't have to do that and as far as I know, as far as anybody knows, Toby never took another man's woman. She was free. You'd better stress that, because Toby had good reason not to take another man's wife . . . somebody took his. But the people who know that don't need to be told and the ones that don't know it don't need to know. Just say that the women he loved, he loved right, and they will know what you mean."

"Mrs. Snow . . . this is rather unusual."

"Now listen . . ." Roxie leaned forward, the anger in her eyes, "are you going to tell it like it was or are you going to come out with a lot of garbage?"

"I'm going to tell it the way you ask me to."

"All right . . . you do that. He was weak and he was strong. He loved people. That street will go on down there, New Hope Street, just like it has, like maybe forever, but Toby will be missing, and for a lot of people, they'll think about him and some of the time they will laugh at the things he did and sometimes they will feel empty because maybe there isn't a Toby around to unload on. Now you tell them all of that, hear? All right."

"Yes . . . I will say those things."

"And make it short. There will be at least a half a dozen drunks in there and they'll be needing to get out for a shot after a few minutes. And none of this nigger crying . . . don't try to make them cry. Toby wouldn't like that at all."

"About ten minutes, Mrs. Snow, if that seems reasonable."

"Yeah . . . ten minutes."

Roxie got up.

"One more thing. Don't read out of the Bible very much. That would embarrass Toby. He never talked much about God." She moved slowly to the study door, placed her hand on the knob, and paused, not turning. "But I'll bet you one thing . . . if there *is* one, by Jesus, he knows it now."

She wore a black veil, a contrast against her neck, the filmy material giving her face a sense of mystery, and a modest black dress beneath which she very deliberately had worn the French bra he had given her when he was being expansive, happy those days, and the bikini panties, as though she wanted him to know. Levi held the door of the funeral car and she saw a glimpse of herself, a reflection in the black shining door as it swung open. Levi got in and one of the funeral directors closed the door. They sat in almost the exact spot where Sonny Hutto had parked his car when he went upstairs to murder Toby.

The people on the street paused to look, some of them openly and others furtively. The kid had gone ahead, perhaps feeling that he would be intruding, though she had told him he was welcome to come with them, that Toby would have approved. An old man with a cane stopped and removed his hat, a tired old dirty felt which he held across his breast, his bald black head now shining in the fall sunlight.

Levi patted her hand gently on the seat as the driver accelerated. "You all right?" he asked.

She did not reply. She had taken one of the last four red pills an hour before and her mind was lured to a kind of indifference, a sweet dullness that she trusted would get her through the ordeal. As the car swept along, several approaching automobiles slowed and pulled to the side until the limousine passed. Roxie leaned her head back against the seat and caught glimpses of the autumn colors of the leaves, dying too, so lovely in these last moments before the rain came to make them heavy, too heavy, releasing them to fall soundlessly to the ground to rot.

The car turned a corner and she saw the hearse parked in front of the church, big and cumbersome, it seemed from the rear, the doors closed, large doors which would open like massive jaws to swallow the coffin she had selected for him. The car stopped behind the hearse as a patrolman, smartly dressed in his uniform, waved them in. And she felt somehow proud as she saw him there. They did that for the important white people over at the Dorchester Baptist Church, sent a motorcycle patrolman to escort the procession, but not very often for . . . but she didn't want to think about that now.

In a moment the door was opened for her. The black man in a fine dark suit nodded gravely and she got out, taking care to be modest with the skirt. Quickly Levi was at her side, taking her arm as they began to climb the steps, and she felt the warmth of the sunshine on her shoulders, the dancing rays of light almost like small spotlights coming through the leaves of the oak trees that grew in front of the old brick church.

She heard the organ as they reached the landing. The black hand of the director swept past her and the door opened. Inside the sanctuary she faced the backs of their heads and hesitated before going down the long aisle, as the organ chords vibrated, it seemed, inside of her. She lifted her head and moved her throat as they started down the aisle, seeing the police officers sitting in a pew together near the back, and she almost smiled, thinking Toby would say it would be a good time to rob any store in town with that much of the force occupied with . . . and saw some of the white businessmen for whom Toby had painted signs regularly. *If you can make a good S, you can make a good living.*

And the women . . . they were there, yes, perhaps remembering the touch of those hands. And some of the men he drank with, some who had hit him for the price of a bottle at the liquor store, the seventy-cent wine, probably shaking inside now but here to say good-by.

As she neared the altar her eyes came upon the casket and she faltered, an involuntary muscular response, but Levi had known perhaps she would because his hand tightened against her arm to overcome the reluctance. As the organ wailed, she reached the pew and saw old Julius and the kid together in the pew behind. She sat and drew in a deep breath which she let out slowly, studying the shiny surface of the casket, closed as she had asked, because Toby would have preferred it that way, would have been miserable if he thought they would all file past the way they did sometimes, weeping into his dead face or leaning into the box to press their lips on the lifeless skin . . . closed to the world now, gone to be seen no more. It did not seem possible. She knew it but she did not yet feel it. *A woman knows a lot of things she doesn't feel.* Yes . . . she remembered. *Beautiful,* he had said.

She heard a cough come from the congregation, from a distance it seemed, from far across a lake on a summer morning, and only then she realized that the organ was silent. In a moment she sensed a movement from above, at the pulpit. She looked up to see the young preacher and she wasn't sure what he was going to do.

He leaned against the wooden altar, his eyes lowered to the casket for a long moment as silence came to the sanctuary. Slowly his eyes lifted, met hers briefly, and swept from side to side as he searched out the faces of the people, as a small smile came to his lips, a kind of wry, almost boyish grin, and the mouth moved as the sounds of his voice, deep and rich, rang out to every corner of the church. He said, "Toby Snow was a hell of a man, now wasn't he?"

Then she knew he was going to come through and he did. She sat there almost smiling as a tear crept along her cheek. They heard, all of them, what they knew of Toby, what they knew him to be, and there was a ripple of laughter somehow turning to mourning when he told of the day Toby threw the brick through the glass just to hear it crash, and that strange sound swept through the church again near the end when the preacher said that he was a sign painter and a good one and referred to that one, the particular one they still talked about . . . and he said on that occasion a great many people had remarked about the special sign he had painted . . . most unusual.

Soon it was over and the mourners filed out silently, or almost silently. She and Levi and the kid lingered for a moment and the preacher said a short prayer for them which she heard but did not hear, and she looked at the casket and remembered . . . remembered.

As they came out into the sunshine again, the mourners gathered at the bottom of the church steps looked gravely up at them. Levi guided her down and in a moment she was inside the limousine. Levi could not or did not feel like speaking, but when the casket appeared at the top of the steps, a groaning sound came from his throat. The people moved back to let the body pass, the faces locked in solemn expressions. The doors of the hearse opened and they clumsily managed to slide the casket inside, shaking his body, and as the doors closed she heard the rumble of the motorcycle in front of the procession. The automobiles had gathered behind, the lights turned on, and the procession began to move forward slowly. As she glanced at the people left behind, she saw the face of a woman who stared at the hearse, not weeping but thoughtful, perhaps one of the women he had known in his life, a woman who had known his touch. In the face she saw nothing at all but the tightly closed teeth and the eyes intent on the black carriage.

The procession turned into the gravel drive of the cemetery, slowly, the tires heavy on the rock, grinding it down into the earth below, a kind of muffled rumble, and stopped at the tent placed above the mound of red earth almost covered by plastic grass blankets. She walked to a bench beside the open grave and sat listening to the soft murmurs of those who had come this far with his body, as they gathered behind her. Levi took her hand and held it lightly in his as the casket, gleaming in the sunshine, was carried to the tent, to the grave beside his son. As she heard the preacher ask God to receive his soul, she looked over the casket to the hedges at the far end of the cemetery, over the other graves, the weathered stones to the small city, and saw the top of the bank building, the courthouse on the square, a fine line of smoke in a windless sky, from the mill smokestack, going up, up until somehow it disappeared. Just gone into nothing.

She did not know it was over until Levi cupped his hand under her elbow. "Roxanne," he said and no more. She stood and let him take her to the car.

When the limousine stopped on New Hope Street, Levi led her up the stairway and to the room. She asked him to leave her alone for a while. She lay on the bed, still in her mourning dress, smelling the foods they had brought, for which she had no appetite. The hours passed slowly. Once she stood, touching the radio, the hot plate, the small refrigerator, and ended at the fruit box nailed to the wall where he had kept his whiskey and cigarettes and his teeth when he took them out. *The life experience,* he had said once. *That was what it was all about.* Well, he'd had that. He damned sure did . . . more often clobbered than triumphant, but he'd lived it. He'd made the scene—all the way.

In the afternoon, as the sun shifted, casting warmth into the room, she called the man in Charlotte. His secretary said she'd see if he was in, and Roxie told her, "Listen, baby . . . he wants a painting down here in Yorksboro bad . . . and if he don't want to talk on the phone, that's his problem, but you tell him the man is dead and if he wants it he better let me know."

The collector came that evening. A distinguished man, a quiet man, the way Toby was, and she thought she understood why he wanted the painting. She led him up the stairs where the painting had been taken and turned on the light and he stood with his hat in his hand for a long while, looking from the painting of the doll tossed in the garbage can to the one of her, and at last he said, "I'd like to buy them both. He hadn't done this one . . . of you."

"For the museum?"

"Yes. I'd like them both."

"How much?"

"We had agreed on a price for the doll. I could make you an offer for both."

"I know about the doll . . . about the other one?"

"Two hundred," he said.

The money didn't matter. It hadn't even been important to ask. The thing was the museum and what Toby would want. She folded her hands across her breasts and looked at the image of herself, the way Toby had seen her, had known her.

She shook her head. "No," she said.

"You're sure?"

"Yeah . . . that was for me."

"I understand. If you ever change your mind . . ."

"Yeah. I know where you are."

He wrote out a check and she stared at the painting of the doll and imagined it in a museum someplace, someday, beside others and wondered at the people who would see it. She heard him tear the check from the pad and accepted it, not looking, watching him lift the frame from the wall.

"Thank you, Mrs. Snow."

She nodded and looked at the bare spot, and then he was gone. That's what Toby wanted. And she had kept the promise. She turned off the light and lay for a moment before getting up in the darkness to feel in the fruit box for the vial of red pills. She took one at the sink and undressed slowly. Nude, she crawled into the bed they had shared and lay looking out the window toward the light behind the used clothing store that glowed but no longer shined into the room because of the shield the old man had put there for Toby. And heard the steady pounding of the bass notes in the bar below, coming through the walls like a distant heartbeat. Her eyes grew heavy from the drug. The glow from the light outside behind the store was cold. Nothing moved. The frantic moths darting and circling with such excitement were gone.

17

Roxie went down to the bar the next afternoon. It was Friday and a lot of paychecks had come in, so the place was crowded and noisy. The juke box was crying out *Baby, baby* . . . and she sat numb, listening, sitting in a small booth, and looked up when the bartender came over and put a glass and a can of beer in front of her. She reached for her purse and he put his hand on hers, stopping the motion, and then he walked away.

She sipped the beer slowly, staring, not seeing anything really but vague moving bodies, hearing laughter and the overriding cry of the juke box . . . *Baby, baby* . . .

The young stud was sitting across from her before she realized it and he said he'd like to buy her a drink. She looked at him . . . young, twenty-eight, probably had a job at the mill and had bought him a nice new car and thought he knew what it was all about.

The beer came and he kept flashing those teeth and telling her what a doll she was, and she knew he'd never heard of Toby Snow, didn't know anything . . . and after a while he touched her hand across the table and she raised her eyes.

"Baby, you sure are quiet," he said.

She looked down and lifted the glass of beer and tasted it. How many . . . three or four now. She was feeling the beer.

He said, "Baby, I'd like for us to go someplace and have a good time."

She met his eyes squarely. She took out a cigarette and his black hand came across the table and touched the flame to the tip. She exhaled slowly, still staring him fiercely in the eyes. And slowly she said, "Twenty dollars."

She watched his head cock to one side, like he was surprised, but in an instant he spread a lascivious grin across his face and nodded. "Where we goin', baby?"

"It's not far."

She got up and, not looking back, knew that shiny new suit was stepping it out behind her. She made him keep a fast pace to the stairway, leading him swiftly up until she reached the door. She opened it and let him inside. His eye caught the painting.

"Say, baby, that's good. That's really you turned on."

In a moment she had draped her dress across the wooden chair and was on her back waiting for him.

He came to her and when he was with her she looked over his shoulder, as he began to labor, and saw the painting and remembered . . . and told this young stud to touch her here, then there . . . which he did. And then, seeing the painting he had done of her, she closed her eyes and tried . . . tried to recapture it and her mind was almost strong enough at one moment to bring it back, but then her mind failed her. He was gone. That was a thing they had had . . . and probably the only thing like that she would ever know and it was gone. So she stopped trying and threw it to him like cracking a whip until he couldn't resist that power.

He dressed casually, looking cocky, like he knew what he was and that he had really turned her on. The stupid bastard. When he reached the door she spoke from the bed.

"Tell your friends," she said.

He nodded. "You can believe that, baby."

Then he closed the door.

Roxanne looked at the painting. She had been that way to a man once. Maybe once was all you got. Maybe it was more than most people ever have. Maybe they spend all their lives not knowing a Toby or feeling the way she felt when she was with him. She left the bed and reached for her dress, thinking again that she had to accept that he was gone and she was alone.

She went to the door and zipped the dress.

"Well, sweetpot," she said softly and nearly choked, feeling the pressure inside as the muscles tightened hard in her stomach . . . but it passed and she stood with her hand on the doorknob and lifted her head. She drew a deep breath and exhaled slowly, feeling the pounding of the bass notes in her feet, notes without melody, just a perfect steady beat. And she thought bitterly there had to be a hundred dollars waiting in that bar and, with a little goddamned luck, not a single case of clap.

She turned the doorknob, the metal growing warm from her hand, and stepped into the hallway. She took a cigarette, hesitating there, touched the flame to the tip, and exhaled a long gray tube of smoke that disappeared into nothing. Simply gone.

She went down the stairs slowly, unbuttoning the top button of her dress so that the lace of the bra and a glimpse of the cleavage would show.

With a few more drinks, hell, she could make it.

A Note About the Author

Robert O'Neil Bristow was born in St. Louis, Missouri, in 1926, and grew up in Oklahoma City, Oklahoma. Following his discharge from the United States Navy, he studied journalism at the University of Oklahoma, from which he was graduated in 1951. For the next several years he earned his living by writing, selling some 135 articles and stories to forty different magazines. In the course of his work he was bitten by a rattlesnake and threatened by a state official he was about to expose. For a year he delivered sermons at the A.M.E. Pleasant Chapel Church in Altus, Oklahoma.

In 1960 Mr. Bristow returned to the University of Oklahoma for a master's degree in journalism. He then accepted an appointment to teach creative writing courses as writer-in-residence at Winthrop College, the South Carolina College for Women, in Rock Hill, where he now lives with his wife, the former Gaylon Walker, and their four children. His first novel, *Time for Glory*, won the University of Oklahoma Award for Literary Excellence for 1969.